I0545604

Arrange Me

KATY REGNERY

Please visit my website at **www.katyregnery.com**
Editors: Tessa Shapcott + Scribe, Inc.
Formatter: CookieLynn Publishing Services
Cover Designer: Katy Regnery

First Edition: March 2019
Arrange Me: a novel / by Katy Regnery—1st ed.
ISBN: 978-1-944810-41-2

My name is Courtney Jane Salinger—
and I'm sick of games.

Sick of the Friday night bar-scene-cum meat market.
Sick of the boy-girl, man-woman, Mars-Venus, flirtation-without-
expectation, game-playing nonsense.
Sick of awful dates and one-night stands, booty calls and guys who
don't call back, mixed messages or NO messages and—and—
and—I'm sick of all of it.

I'm done.
I just can't do it anymore.
It's too hard, and even worse: little by little, it's making *me* hard.
It's breaking my heart.

What *do* I want?
That's easy.

I want a house in suburbia with a white picket fence.
I want babies to buckle into a minivan.
But most of all, I want to be married.
I want a husband.

So I've made an important decision: I'm making my escape from
the dating world and the single life.
I've filled out my application on ArrangeMe.com and I'm putting
my fate into the hands of experts.

Is it a little scary?
Sure.
I mean, I have no idea who I'll end up with.
After all, I'm planning to marry a complete stranger.

But between you and me?
I can't wait.

Being arranged can't possibly be worse than being single.
Can it?

For Mia.
Your constant and faithful friendship makes this
author journey the best adventure ever.
I adore you.
#NoSpace

***

Kind thanks to Nidhi Agarwal, Ritu Pandulla, Suvitha Ramaswamy,
and Sonal Dutt for their help in calibrating Dina's character.

Arrange Me

PROLOGUE

I saw a movie once.

I think it took place in the Middle Ages…or maybe Viking times? I'm not sure, but I *do* know one thing for certain: in the movie, there was an arranged marriage. A man loyal to the king of England, but without land or wealth, was betrothed to a woman who had both.

The man started his day bathing in a lake, long hair braided behind his ears to keep it out of his face but shaggy and loose down his back. When he turned toward the camera, his eyes were bright blue. Clear blue. Like the summer sky or raspberry shaved ice. Maybe twenty-two years old, he was beautiful standing in that lake with beads of water shining on his bare chest.

In the next scene, a woman arrived on horseback at a stone church in the middle of a walled village. She wore a simple blue dress with a white collar. She wasn't too tall or too short; she wasn't fat or thin. She was about as average as could be except for one thing: over her face, she wore a black veil that reminded me of the veil on a beekeeper's hat. Very dark, and thick enough that a bee's stinger couldn't get through the mesh, the veil hid her face completely.

The man from the lake reappears, now dressed in his

shabby best. He helps her dismount, offers her his arm, and together they walk into the church.

They're *literally* about to get married.

But he's never seen her, and she's never seen him.

For all he knows, she could be one hundred years old. Or she could be young and homely. Her teeth could be rotten brown stubs. She could be disfigured or—or hell, behind those plain yet generous skirts and thick veil, she could even be a boy. Not to mention whatever might be under the clothes and inside the skin. My God, what a crapshoot. She could be insane or extremely unreasonable, mealy mouthed or childlike. She could have a razor-sharp tongue or collect—I don't know—creepy dolls or have terrible gas or, worst of the worst, she could be a genuinely black-hearted person.

There is no way for him to know what's behind the veil.

There is no way for him to know to whom he is about to bind his life.

A priest tells them to hold hands, and they do.

But just before she gives her vows, she reaches for her veil, and—

Ooof.

An elbow in my side brings me swiftly back to reality.

"You don't have to do this," my aunt hisses, her breath hot on the shell of my ear. "This is craziness, Courtney. Utter insanity."

I clench my teeth together. Hard.

"I love you, Aunt Lucy, but you don't have to stay."

"I'm not leaving." She takes my hand in a death grip.

"But there is absolutely no reason for you to do this! Darling, reconsider—"

"Please, Aunt Lucy," I bite out.

"We can turn around right now," she continues, her tone passing panic and veering into hysteria. "Run out of here. The car's waiting in the parking lot. We'll drive straight to the airport. We could just—"

"No."

I try to take a deep breath, which reminds me that I'm in a corseted white dress. I must have been stress eating over the past two weeks, because it's tight around my lungs and I can't fill them completely.

"You can still change your mind," she insists with tears in her voice.

"No."

"*Please* don't do this," she begs me in a thin whisper.

My toes are pinched in my brand-new, too-small, white satin kitten heels. I feel a bead of sweat start at the nape of my neck, just below a careful updo, and make its way down my spine, which is covered in white lace.

My left hand matches her grip as I clench a small bouquet of white calla lilies in my right.

Suddenly, at the very moment when I *might* have reconsidered what I am about to do, I hear Pachelbel's Canon in D start playing just inside the small church. Not a second later, the ancient, dark-wood doors before us whoosh open.

I gasp softly, instantly turning my gaze downward to the threadbare red carpeting that runs from the narthex to the altar.

To calm myself, I think of the man in the movie.

Taking my first step down the aisle, I wonder: *How many others have done the same in this very place—married someone they'd never met before?*

One step. Another.

It probably worked out fine for them, I tell myself.

Step together. Step.

It's time, Courtney. Look up.

Step together. Step.

For God's sake, Courtney Jane! You wanted this. You chose this. Now, have courage and look up, goddamnit!

Nearly halfway down the aisle, I raise my chin, but only enough to see the Presbyterian minister's cream-colored robe, embroidered with gold crosses. Peripherally, to his left, I can see the form of a man.

"I'll be the one in the penguin suit."

"It's not too late!" my aunt sobs softly, squeezing the blood from my hand.

In defiance of her words, I lift my head all the way.

My breath catches.

My lips pop open.

My heart stops beating.

As—

finally, finally, finally

—I look into the eyes of my future husband.

CHAPTER 1

Six Weeks Ago

<u>Courtney</u>

"If I have one more crappy date, I'll kill myself."

Dina, my friend from work, laughs at me. "If every girl killed herself after every crappy date, the world would be empty."

"*Half* empty," I say, gesturing to the bartender for another gimlet. I glance at Dina. "You sticking with beer?"

"Yep."

Josh-the-charming-bartender stops in front of me and grins. "Another round?"

"Keep 'em coming."

"Bad week?" he asks, making a sad-puppy face.

"Bad life."

"How about you?" he asks Dina, leaning forward a touch.

I swear to Christ. These two. They've been playing this flirty cat-and-mouse game for over a year.

"Nope. I'm all good," she says in a lower voice than normal.

"Hell yes you are, Hot Stuff."

I don't have enough energy for the number of eyerolls

this exchange deserves. I rap my empty glass on the chrome bar. "Hey! I'm empty."

"Hold your horses," says Josh, swatting me away like a gnat. He turns back to Dina. "What happened with that guy from last weekend?"

"Wouldn't you like to know?" she asks, licking her lips.

He bites his lower lip. "I love a good bedtime story."

She chuckles, and it's this sexy, throaty sound that some girls can pull off and some can't. Dina can pull it off. Me? No way. I'd sound like I had laryngitis, and some well-intentioned grandmother-type would likely tap me on the shoulder to offer me a lozenge.

I hold out my glass. "Dying...of...thirst. So...very...parched."

"My bestie needs a drink," says Dina, giving her beer bottle a quick blow job to finish the swill before offering the now-empty phallus to Josh. "Do your job for a change."

"Tease," he growls, winking at me before turning his back to refill our drinks.

"Why don't you two just *do it* already?" I ask her.

Dina laughs, but the sound is lighter and higher now. She's back to her normal, non-bitch-in-heat self. "With Josh? Ha. No. No way! Josh is just...you know, fun. It's just a game, our back-and-forth."

"Couldn't it be more?" I ask.

"Nuh-uh. He's not my type." She shrugs, turning around on her stool to look at the crowd of Wall Street–types that populates this particular Battery Park bar. I join her to find a vast sea of dark-blue blazers and dark-gray suits.

White and light-blue dress shirts abound. Here and there you get someone with a little personality—a jaunty red tie or a daring purple pocket square. But mostly the uniform is the same. Some of the men are blond, some brunette; some are Asian, some black. Virtually every ethnicity is represented, and they all reek of Justice Kavanaugh–style prep school shenanigans.

Once upon a time, I looked forward to after-work drinks with Dina at Tidewaters Bar & Grille. But after five years? I'm over it. I'm so over it, if "it" were sex, I would find the nearest nunnery and check in ASAP.

Except I like sex. A lot. I just wish I could find a steady partner.

"That'll be nineteen-fifty."

I twist back around. "Put it on my tab."

Josh gestures toward Dina, who's flirting with the nearest bond trader, with a flick of his chin. "Flavor of the night?"

"Definitely." I tilt my head to the side and look at Josh objectively as he helps another customer.

Aside from being my favorite bartender, he's good-looking. Like, movie-star-*hot* good-looking. Like, take a second-, third-, and fourth-look good-looking. Like, way-out-of-my-league good-looking.

With dark-brown hair and light-blue eyes, he has this Ian Somerhalder thing going on, only he's not smirky and doesn't look like he wants to suck my blood. He's super sexy but in a less dangerous and more charming way, if that makes any sense.

That said, I don't fawn all over Josh like most of the girls who walk in here, and he doesn't flirt with me like I'm a moron with half a brain. I look forward to chatting with him, and he always has a cold gimlet waiting for me.

"Why haven't you ever asked her out?" I ask him.

"Dina? She wouldn't say yes," he says, grinning at me. "Besides, she's not my type."

She's not my type.

It's enough to make my head explode. "So, you two flirt…every single Friday night…for no reason at all?"

"Not for *no* reason. It's fun."

"Fun." I release an exasperated breath, thinking about my last in a series of terrible dates. Dan.

Dan, Dan, the Stockbroker Man, who had his hands down my shirt before the cab even left the curb in front of the restaurant where we'd had dinner. When I pushed him away and told him I didn't make out on the first date, he called me a "frosty bitch" and a "waste of time."

So maybe it's thoughts of slimeball Dan, or maybe it's the fact that I'm on my fourth drink, but suddenly I hear myself saying with absolute and total honesty, "I just don't understand."

Josh nods at a guy standing behind me and shifts slightly to his right to pull a pint of beer from the tap.

"What don't you understand?" he asks.

"All of this," I mutter with disgust. I pluck the straw from my drink because…more alcohol. Stat.

"All of *what?*" He puts the beer next to my elbow, and a twenty-dollar bill quickly replaces it.

"*This!*" I toss a thumb over my shoulder. "This meat market. This boy-girl, man-woman, flirtation-without-expectation, I-buy-you-dinner-you-put-out, game-playing bullshit."

He raises his eyebrows at me. "Whoa. I'm—"

"It's all a *game,* but it's not *fun,*" I insist, on a genuine rant now. "It sucks." I prop my elbows on the bar as Josh mixes a martini for the woman sitting on a barstool next to me. "You play hard to get, they want you. You act like you want them, they don't want you back. Everyone around me's speaking a language I don't understand!"

He grins. "I think that's just the ongoing battle of the sexes. Me, Tarzan. You, Jane."

"Gah! I don't want a caveman," I moan. "I just...I want the real thing. I'm done with shitty dates and one-night stands and booty calls and guys who don't call back and mixed messages, or *no* messages, and—and—and all of it. I'm done. I just want..."

"What?"

"Marriage," I blurt out.

He recoils. "Marriage?"

Wait. What? Is that *what I really want? Marriage?*

I picture a little house in Connecticut like the one I grew up in, with a big oak tree in the back and a white picket fence around the front. Some sweet guy wearing jeans and a T-shirt is mowing the lawn with his back to me. A couple of kids come running out of the house and climb into the minivan and—

"You know what?" I say, the crazy idea gaining steam

in my head. "Yeah. Marriage. I'd like to skip all of *this* crap and cut to the chase."

"Marriage," he says softly, staring at me intently like I'm teaching him a new word. In Swahili.

"Yeah. I think that would be nice," I say, finishing the rest of my gimlet. "Cash me out, huh?"

His gaze drifts over to Dina, who's draped over her Judge Brett doppelgänger like an expensive pashmina. Then he looks back at me. "You're leaving?"

"Yes. Yes, I am. I'm going home. I'm going to go home and figure this out."

"How to get married."

"Exactly."

"After four gimlets."

"No time like the present."

"And what about her? You're her wingman."

"She won't even notice I'm gone. But! If she's solo at last call," I pluck a twenty from my wallet and place it on the bar, "make sure she gets into a cab, huh?"

He slides my card to me. I sign the receipt with a flourish before looking up to find Josh-the-bartender staring at me. Slowly, a grin spreads across his face, and it warms me in the weirdest way, because it makes him feel new to me. And for a split second, I think he's a little surprised he never noticed before now how very new *I* am.

"Good luck, Courtney," he says, his voice soft and earnest.

"Thank you, Josh."

I grab my coat and purse, waggle my fingers good-bye,

and walk straight through that sea of suits to the nearest exit.

***

On the short walk home, I stare out at the Hudson River, pulling my coat tighter over my chest as the wind whips up a little across the water. It's April in New York City, which can offer sunny skies one day and snow flurries the next. Not that it's actually going to snow tonight, but it's a chilly fifty degrees by the water, so I speed up my steps, thinking about my conversation with Josh.

Marriage.

Hmm.

I have no idea what made me tell Josh-the-bartender my deepest desire—*I'm ignoring you, four gimlets*—but there it is: marriage. To meet someone nice, get married, and live happily ever after. Why can't it be that easy? Why the hell does it have to be so hard?

Sighing as I arrive at my building, I walk in and give the concierge a small wave as I beeline to the elevator and press sixteen.

My one-bedroom apartment is snug, but the building has a gym overlooking the Hudson, a pool on the roof, and a small lawn where you can sit in the sun on summer Sundays and read a book.

Not that I work out much, swim often, or have a lot of time for reading.

I've been with the same financial firm—DeWitt, Morris & Jones—for five years, ever since I graduated from the University of Rochester with my MFE. And frankly, they keep me pretty busy.

I unlock my apartment door and step inside, feeling, as I always do, a deep sense of satisfaction at being home. Here in my sanctuary, which I paid for on my own, all the hustle and noise of the city melts away, and on a night like tonight—*a Friday, thanks be to God*—all I want to do is kick off my heels, change into pajamas, pour myself a glass of wine, and watch bad TV.

As I walk by the remote, I pick it up, press "ON," and then throw it on the couch as I head down the short hallway that leads to my bedroom and bathroom.

I can hear the chatter of a talk show or reality program as I toe off my shoes and unzip my knee-length camel skirt. I throw it in the bag to be dry-cleaned, my silk blouse and black cashmere cardigan quickly following it. I unclasp my bra, mewling with pleasure as my size-C breasts are released after long hours of confinement.

Opening my dresser drawer, I pull out a Haverford College T-shirt and pull it over my head, and then I open a second drawer to grab some black Yoga pants, which I tug on while I walk barefooted back to the living room.

"Why did I want to be married at first sight?"

I stop in my tracks, looking up at the twentysomething guy being interviewed on the plasma screen.

"I guess I'm ready to meet 'the one.' I'm ready to get serious. Have kids. The whole thing." He pauses, a sweet smile spreading across his lips before he continues: "You know what? I can't wait to meet my future wife."

My mouth is hanging open as the show cuts to a commercial—an announcer promising us that we'll meet the man's arranged match, Simone, as soon as the program returns.

I can't wait to meet my future wife.

Yes, I think. *Yes, yes, yes! This is what I'm talking about!*

Hurrying to the kitchen to pour myself a large glass of wine before the show resumes, I grab my laptop from its charger on the kitchen counter and hustle back into the living room just as another commercial begins. A preppy-looking blond man is standing in a backyard, a bright-green lawn and children's swing set behind him.

"Are you a fan of Lifetime's hit reality show *Arrange Me*? Well, now you can meet your future spouse at the altar too!"

Slowly, transfixed by the man speaking, I lower my body to the couch, letting my laptop slide back through my arm and onto a cushion as I raise my wineglass to my mouth and take a huge gulp.

"After my experience on the show, I decided that it wasn't fair for the viewers at home not to experience the level of matchmaking expertise from which I—and my wife, Jen—were able to benefit."

He walks over to a gorgeous redheaded woman helping a strawberry-blonde baby take steps across the pristine green lawn.

"You probably recognize us from season four, right?" she asks, swooping up the baby into her arms. She stands beside her handsome husband and beams at the camera. "But did you know that this little bundle of joy arrived exactly nine months after filming wrapped?" She kisses the baby before smiling at her husband. "Baby Casey made us a family. Brad and I couldn't be happier."

"That's right, Jen. And it couldn't have happened without the help of our new best friends: relationship guru Dr. Jake, spiritual advisor Pastor Ken, and sex expert Dr. Sydney Morningstar."

Pictures of said experts flash across the screen, and with intense concentration, I stare at their faces while wondering about the magic they are somehow able to procure.

Happy Jen giggles demurely when Brad says "sex expert," and I find myself chuckling along with her like she's my long-lost BFF and I *totes* get where she's coming from.

Back to Brad, who says, "For only $399, payable by credit card, we will send you the same thirty-page application that we had to fill out before we were successfully matched."

"That's right! Then *your* information will be sent to the same experts who matched *us!* Once they find your perfect mate in the Arrange Me Too database, they will put you two in touch. The rest is up to you!"

"Isn't it time to leave the rat race to the rats?" Brad chuckles as he puts an arm around Jen's shoulder and pulls her closer. "What have you got to lose? Log in to www.arrange-me-too.com, and start the process today!"

"And maybe," says Jen, propping up the baby so their three adorable, happy-family faces take up the whole screen, "you'll find your very own happy ending—"

"Just like us," finishes Brad, turning her and Casey away from the camera to walk across their perfect yard and leaving the website address in bright white lettering for viewers.

I blink only when the theme song to *Arrange Me* returns, and suddenly we're at the bridal salon with Simone, who's choosing her perfect wedding dress under the disapproving gaze of her mother and sister.

Placing my wineglass on the coffee table in front of me, I grab my laptop, flip it open, and type in the website address for Arrange Me Too, my knee bouncing with excitement as the site comes up.

Suddenly, Brad and Jen's happy faces are smiling back at me, with smaller pictures of the three experts just below.

"Ready to Get Married?"

I click on the tab, biting my bottom lip as another screen appears, this one with a list of instructions and another button to click on:

"Pay $399 Now to Start the Process!"

I pause for a second, my father's shark-in-the-boardroom genes no doubt asserting themselves as I consider paying almost four hundred dollars for something that isn't guaranteed. But four gimlets and half a glass of New Zealand Sauvignon Blanc are determined to have their way. I click on the tab and upload my credit card information.

"Fill Out Your Application!"

I take another big gulp of wine as Simone declares a heavily beaded, Cinderella-style ball gown "the dress" and then refill my glass before clicking on the tab and waiting for the form to download.

CHAPTER 2

<u>Josh</u>

Marriage.

What an inappropriate fucking word to say during happy hour at the sleaziest high-end bar that New York's hallowed financial district has to offer.

I watch her weave her way through the many Wall Street douchebags in the crowd, feeling vaguely wistful when the front door closes behind her.

Courtney Jane Salinger.

I've been cashing her out for over a year now, and not only is she a consistently good tipper, she's a sweetheart too.

Her hair is blonde, and her eyes are blue, and she's curvier than her friend, Dina. She looks like she comes from money, which I'm pretty sure she does. I've heard her talk about spending weekends at her parents' house in Greenwich, and after an absence of two Fridays last summer, she came back from Nantucket with a respectable tan. But she doesn't dress like a shark or a super model. She's more about skirts and cardigans than power suits. Like I said, cute.

She's also a lot chattier than her friend. And as any bartender can tell you, you can learn a ton about your regulars with a little strategic eavesdropping. She likes her job but isn't crazy about her boss, who is sometimes "handsy." She lives in a building with a view of the Hudson, and when she sneezes, it actually sounds like "ah-choo!" She's kind to everyone, though I've also heard her take down a Wall Street asshole with a clever one-liner.

I like Courtney. Always have.

Not to mention her surname is Salinger, and I have wondered about a million times if she's related to one of my heroes, J. D. Salinger. Maybe someday I'll figure out a way to ask her that won't sound completely opportunistic.

I'm going to go home and figure this out.

I'm chuckling about it as the cougar at the end of the bar flashes a "fuck-me" smile in my general direction and lifts her empty wineglass. She's hot. No question. But I don't fuck the customers. Concealing a sigh, I cash out a guy near the tap before heading her way.

"What can I get for you?" I ask.

"Another glass," she purrs, "and your phone number."

"You're drinking the cab, right?"

"Mm-hm."

I pull the bottle from under the bar and fill her glass.

"That'll be fourteen dollars."

"And how much for the digits?" she asks, placing a twenty on the bar.

I take the bill. "Change?"

She shrugs, her expression starting to cool. "Depends."

Oh, man. She's persistent.

I take the twenty to the register, then place six dollars in front of her before looking up.

She narrows her eyes at me. "So that's a no?"

I don't know what to say. Awkward shit like this will be the first thing I *don't* miss when I quit this job someday. I don't want to hurt her feelings, and she's a good-looking woman, but no, I'm not interested. Do I need to spell it out in neon?

"Sorry."

"Girlfriend?" she asks.

"Pardon?"

"The blonde chick with the sizeable ass. Your girlfriend?"

Sizeable ass? Courtney? Huh. I've never thought of her as overweight. She's not skinny, but she's not "sizeable" either. What's interesting, however, is that instead of telling myself this woman is entitled to her opinion and walking away, I find myself doing something I'm not supposed to— something I never do. Instead of turning away to help another customer, I engage.

Placing both hands on the bar between us, I ask, "What if she is?"

"You can do better."

"Can I?"

She nods. "Aw, sweetheart. Of course you can. In case nobody ever told you, you're hot. You're young. Your eyes are moderately sharp."

Moderately? What a fucking bitch.

"What do you do, honey? Are you an actor?"

I shake my head. "No."

"Well, whatever you are, you shouldn't settle for her. Whatever she's got, someone else has got it better. A *lot* better. I can guarantee you."

"You've never even met her."

"So? I know her type: Grew up in the suburbs. Went to some liberal arts college. Works at a financial firm. As soon as she meets the right guy, she'll be driving the soccer car pool, and that caboose will grow three sizes bigger by the time she's forty." Cougar takes a long sip of the inky red wine. "Is that really what you want? To be stuck with some boring butterball out in suburbia? God. Kill me now."

"Wow," I say, shaking my head back and forth. "You're hardcore."

"You should see me in bed."

"No, thanks."

Her eyes flare, wide and angry.

"Anything else?" I ask, taking a step back and crossing my arms over my chest.

"Yeah," she says softly, offering me a grin so mean and brittle, it's a wonder it isn't the crack that breaks her face. She leans closer. "You're a bartender. A loser. You deserve each other."

It's on the tip of my tongue to call her a washed-up hag, but I need this job…at least for now.

"Yeah. Maybe we do," I say softly, before turning around and heading to the other end of the bar. I'm feeling pissed, so I stop by the cash register to get myself together.

"That was some heavy flirting," says Annie, sidling up beside me while shaking some sort of fruity martini. "Even for you."

"Hardly. She's a bitch."

"Oh, yeah?" asks Annie. "Huh. You usually get along with everyone."

She's right. I usually do, but that woman really got under my skin for some reason. What right does she have to say any of that garbage about Courtney? Fuck her.

"What's going on in that head tonight?" Annie asks me.

I take a deep breath and let it go. "You ever think about getting married, Annie?"

"You asking?" She winks at me. Annie's in her fifties and has a son my age. She's like a surrogate mom to all the guys who work with her at Tidewaters. "No. Been there, done that. I like my freedom."

"Right."

She cocks her head to the side before pouring the pink contents of her shaker into a V-shaped glass. "You even have a girlfriend, Josh?"

"No."

She places a lime twist on the rim and steps toward the bar. "Might want to get one first, huh? Before thinking about marriage?"

I nod before sliding past her to the other end of the bar, where I take three orders in quick succession: four glasses of Chardonnay, an Amstel and a martini, two gin and tonics, and a whiskey sour. More drinks follow those, until Annie nudges me in the side a few hours later.

"It's one o'clock, honey, and I'm on the late shift. You can go."

My feet are tired and my hands are pruney. I'm more than ready to go home, but I know that sometimes Annie babysits her grandson in the morning, and an extra hour of sleep means a lot to her. "I can stay if you want."

Her smile is instantaneous. "You don't mind?"

"Nah," I say. "Take off. I'll see you on Sunday."

She kisses my cheek before heading to the end of the bar and waving good-bye.

It's quieter now, and since we close in an hour, I can start cleaning up. As I look out over the thinning crowd, I see a couple making out in the corner and realize that Dina is still here.

Dina and I have been flirting with each other since the first time she and Courtney walked through the door of Tidewaters last spring, and I have to admit: I always look forward to seeing her. It's fun, just like I told Courtney. But for whatever reason, right this minute, I'm glad that it never went anywhere else. I'm glad it just remained a harmless flirtation.

I come out from behind the bar and walk over to where Dina and Mr. Bond Trader are canoodling.

"Hey, Dina," I say, taking seven empty beer bottles off the table and weaving them between my fingers.

"Josh-eee," she says, pulling away from an intense lip-lock and looking up at me. "Hiiiii!"

Her words are slurred and her lipstick's smeared, but she's in high spirits.

"Hey there. You doing okay? You need a cab? Courtney left twenty bucks so I could grab you one."

"Court-ney! Ohmygod! I looooove her."

"Yeah. She's nice."

"*So nice*! Literally, the nicest *ever*!" Dina agrees, nodding emphatically. "And *you're* nice!"

"Thanks."

"Under all that sex-eeeee-ness, you're the boy next dooooooor."

I smile at her, shaking my head. "Thanks, I guess."

"You know what? Ohmygod, Josheeeee! You should *totally* ask her out."

"Yeah. Okay." I chuckle at her. "How about that cab?"

She looks at the guy sitting next to her, who's wearing half of her fire engine red lipstick around his lips. "You're cute. Who are you again?"

"Chip."

"Riiiiight. Are you takin' me home or what?"

He blinks at her, like he's not entirely certain who she is, but he's not going to let that get in his way. "Yeah. Sure. Okay. Let's go."

His words are about as slurred as hers. A match made in drunken heaven.

***

A week later, I find myself looking up at the door every few minutes, and it finally occurs to me that I'm looking for Courtney Jane Salinger.

There's no point in denying it: I've thought about her and our incredibly weird conversation about *mawidge*—thank you, *Princess Bride*—several times since last Friday. More than anything, I want an update. Was her intention to "go home and figure this out" actualized? Or was it just the gimlets talking? She seemed so determined, I wouldn't be surprised if she walked in tonight with a ring on her finger. As I pour a glass of Chardonnay for a lonely woman standing by the bar, the thought bugs me a little. I hope Courtney doesn't do anything stupid.

"Twelve dollars."

The woman places a twenty on the bar. "Keep the change."

"Thanks." It's only five fifteen, so the crowd is still pretty thin. "Waiting for someone?"

"My fiancé," she says. "He works a few doors down."

"Stockbroker?"

"Mm-hm." She pulls out an empty barstool and sits down. The rock on her finger catches the light, refracting it onto the shiny chrome bar.

"How long have you been engaged?"

"Three months," she says with a sweet smile.

"When's the big day?"

"September." She sighs. "Feels like a long way away."

I nod like I understand, not that I do. I've never even considered what planning a wedding entails. Hell, I've only *been* to a few weddings in my life, and those were when I was young and living at home. Most of my friends here in the city are holdovers from my New York University days, and not many of them are "marriage types." Actors, singers, musicians, and playwrights tend to keep things fluid. You never know when your big break is going to come along and you'll have to pick up stakes to follow your dreams.

"It'll be here before you know it," I say, winking at her.

She takes a sip of her Chardonnay. "Are you an actor?"

I get this all the time. When I was in college, I had a professor who told me I had "the look" and encouraged me to go the acting route instead of the writing route. But my heart was—and still is—in my pen, regardless of how I look on the outside.

"Playwright."

Her eyes widen. "Huh. Interesting. I don't think I've ever met a playwright before."

"We're a dying breed," I say. "Literally."

She chuckles. "Hard knocks?"

"You have no idea," I say, and it's true.

I live in a two-bedroom apartment with four other artists trying to "make it" in the New York theater world, and between the five of us, it's still a struggle to make the $3,000 rent some months. Most of us have other jobs: bartending, waiting tables, coaching, or tutoring, but all of us are living for the dream of seeing our name—or the name of our play—in lights.

"Have I seen anything you've written?"

"Probably not." I shake my head as I take an empty pint glass off the bar and dunk it in a sink of warm, soapy water. "Maybe someday."

"Someday soon?"

I don't actually know how to answer her. I've been a resident playwright at the New Dramatists for five years, ever since graduating with a BA in dramatic writing from the Tisch School at NYU, and the reality is that luck or grace can strike at any time. I know because I've seen it. One of my old roommates, Bryce Turner, was a chorus dancer and understudy actor on Broadway for six years before he was asked to play a lead part one night. Out of the blue. Just like that. And suddenly Bryce could quit his shitty second job as a cashier at Macy's and moved into his own place, because after that, the lead roles just kept on coming.

That's how quickly your luck can change.

"Fingers crossed," I say.

"What's your name?" she asks. "So I can say 'I-knew-you-when.'"

"Josh Dalton."

"Pen name?"

I shake my head. "Nope. Real name. Charles Joshua Dalton, of the Minnetonka Daltons."

"Fancy."

"You ever been to Minnetonka?" I ask, capping her off because she's nice and it's quiet and it's pleasant chatting with her.

"Never."

"Lucky," I say, laughing softly. "Nah, I'm kidding. It's a small town, but it's fine. And most importantly, it had a theater. The Minnetonka Theater. Not a bad venue."

"I bet that's the place where young Josh Dalton's dreams started, huh?"

"That's right."

The door opens, and a blond guy wearing sunglasses and carrying a briefcase stops just inside the vestibule, placing his sunglasses on top of his head and looking around for someone. When he sets his eyes on my Chardonnay-drinking friend, his face lights up, and he beelines over to us.

"I think your fiancé's here."

She turns around and hops off the stool, letting herself be enveloped in his arms and kissed hello.

There's something about watching their reunion that tightens my chest, and my eyes linger on them for an extra second before I turn around to straighten liquor bottles that are already pretty tidy.

What's going on with you, Dalton?

"Hey. How about a gimlet?"

My breath catches as my heart starts to gallop, and a mass of butterflies I haven't felt since high school converges under my ribcage.

Oh, my heart.

Oh, fuck. My heart.

I turn around, and it should be no great surprise to see Courtney Jane Salinger sitting across from me, but somehow it is. Or maybe it's the unexpected pleasure erupting inside of me that's such a surprise. I don't know. I'm not sure.

I am, however, absolutely certain that the partial rewrite of my female lead character in *Miss Gibbons Will See You Now* was based, at least in part, on her.

And when my mom and dad called from Minnetonka to check on their black sheep–playwright son last Sunday, and Mom had asked if there was "anyone special" in my life, Courtney had flashed through my mind for no good reason.

And the idea to add a brand-new scene centered around the word "marriage" in my play *Catching Caufield*? Pretty sure that originated with Courtney and our short, strange conversation last week.

"Are you okay?" Courtney asks, placing her purse on the stool next to her to reserve it for Dina.

"Yeah." I clear my throat. "Uh. Yeah. Fine."

This is a lie.

I'm not fine.

I'm affected by her presence. I'm turned on like a lamp. I'm interested in learning more.

But mostly, I'm…bothered by all of it.

It is absolutely not *fine* with me.

CHAPTER 3

<u>Courtney</u>

The last time I saw Josh-the-hot-bartender, the way he smiled my way had warmed me and made me feel new. But the way he's looking at me right now, like I did something inexcusably rude or unforgivably wrong, gives me the opposite impression. Why does he look so pissed?

"Did—did I shortchange you last week?"

"No," he says, avoiding my eyes. "You said a gimlet, right?"

I've been ordering the same drink almost every Friday night for five years, and the past one with Josh behind the bar. He *knows* what I drink.

"Yeah."

I watch his spare movements as he mixes it for me. Gin. Fresh lime juice. A squeeze of agave. Ice. Shake. Pour.

"Fourteen dollars," he says, placing a navy-blue cocktail napkin on the bar and my drink on top.

I slide my credit card over the shiny chrome. "I'll start a tab."

He takes the card to the register, turning his back to me without another word.

And I know it's stupid, because I really don't know Josh very well outside of my weekly cocktail hour with Dina, but his blatant lack of warmth toward me makes me realize how much I look forward to seeing him every Friday evening. Seeing Josh's welcoming smile has come to represent something important and cherished to me: freedom, the end of the work week, the excitement of the weekend. At some point, a cold drink and warm smile somehow started to mean more to me than a generic bartender-patron exchange, and I don't like being iced out like this. What happened?

"Hey," I say, "is everything okay?"

He turns around but keeps his distance, standing against the shelves lined with bottles instead of laying his hands flat on the bar in front of me and leaning closer to chitchat.

"Yeah. Why?"

I try for a smile, but it feels flat. "You seem…upset."

He crosses his arms over his chest, his cool blue eyes looking into mine. "I'm not."

I've noticed before that Josh has great arms. They're not super ripped or anything, just slightly tanned and nicely toned. But right now? Crossed over his chest? They look strong but unwelcoming, like he's protecting himself from something.

I fumble for another smile. "Okay."

He takes a deep breath, which broadens his chest under his gray T-shirt, then turns and heads down to the end of the bar.

What the hell? Is he just having a bad day, or is it me?

I can't think of anything I've done. I mean, just last week I saw him, paid my tab, and left twenty dollars for Dina's cab. Nothing egregious there.

And I know it's a little egocentric to wonder if I, personally, have anything to do with his bad mood, since we don't know each other all that well, but call it intuition. For whatever reason, it *feels* personal.

"Hey, Courts!" Dina hangs my purse on a hook under the bar and slides onto the stool I've been saving for her.

"Whassup, ladycakes?"

"Josh-the-grouchy-bartender is in a bad mood."

"Really?" She bites her bottom lip as she flicks a look in his direction. "Maybe he's just been missing me."

A bottle of Amstel Light—Dina's drink of choice— appears before us suddenly, but Josh is gone before either of us even looks up or has a chance to say "thank you."

"Thank you!" she calls with a little sass, and Josh nods at her over his shoulder before helping another customer.

"He's being weird, right?"

"Whatevs." Dina lifts the bottle to her lips and takes a long sip. "So, give me the scoop. I haven't seen you since last week. What's been going on?"

Dina was attending a financial conference in Atlanta this week and only returned this afternoon, but she's deluded if she thinks that anything interesting is going on at DeWitt, Morris & Jones. The most exciting thing I can come up with is that there's a new copy machine in accounting.

"Nothing to tell. Same old." I take a sip of my gimlet before turning my legs to face her. "Can I ask you something?"

"Sure. Anything. I'm an open book. You know that."

"You're Indian."

She side-eyes me. "Um, yeah."

"I mean…your parents are *from* India."

"My mother is. My father *technically* is, but he's been here since he was a baby."

"Was their marriage arranged?"

She pulls a hand through her jet-black, glossy hair. "Yep. My mother's family and my father's family go way back. So even though my father's family was already settled here, my grandfathers talked about getting their kids together and…you know, brought my mother over to marry my father."

"Had they ever met?"

"Nope. I mean…yeah, maybe. My father's family went back to India a few times during his childhood, so it's possible they met when they were kids. But once my father started high school, his family didn't go back as much. So if they did meet, it was when they were both young." She takes another gulp of beer. "Put it this way: they definitely didn't *know* each other."

"But they did it anyway. Agreed to the arrangement. Got married. Basically, at first sight."

"Of course. It's tradition. Younger generations have a little more freedom, but my mummy still believes that arranged marriages are the best marriages."

"Are they happy?" I ask.

She shrugs, then grins at me. "Yeah, I think so. He

complains about her cooking. She tells him he's a slob. But they fall asleep together every night."

I sigh because that sounds so nice.

"So…what's with all the questions about my parents?"

"I might have done a thing."

"A good thing or a bad thing?"

"You know that show on Lifetime, *Arrange Me*?"

She rolls her eyes. "Oh, my God! I *hate* that show! People who've never seen each other before get married by supposed *experts*? Sure. I know it. It's crazytown."

Josh stops at the cash register with his back to us, and usually I'd say hi or invite him to join our conversation, but since he's ignoring me, I decide to ignore him too.

"Why do you say that?" I ask her. "Your parents did it."

"No, baby. What my parents did was *totally* different. Night and day."

I scoff. "How so?"

"Their parents were friends from the same caste, from the same town in India. They had a family connection. The families loved their kids and wanted the best for them. Not to mention, the attitude is totally different in India."

"What do you mean?"

"People with arranged marriages there don't *expect* to fall in love at first sight. And they don't expect the match to be perfect. Indians come from this place of having their whole lives to get to know their spouse and *grow* to love them. Marriage itself is the bond—not just the feelings that precede marriage. Let's put it this way: arranged marriage in India isn't just based on feelings. More than that, it's based on mutual respect, family, and commitment. That's why arranged marriages work in India. And that's precisely why they don't work here."

I mull this over for a minute, letting the nuances of what she's saying really sink in, and I conclude that she's probably right. Arranged marriage will have less success in a country where marriage is based, in large part, on love rather than on mutual respect, family, and commitment.

I ask myself if I can let go of my American sensibilities toward marriage and adopt a more Indian approach. Am I ready to commit to someone without knowing the first thing about them? Just because well-intentioned "experts" think we have the potential to be a good match?

Dina raps her long nails on the bar. "Hey! You still haven't told me—what did you do?"

"Well, there's this website called Arrange Me Too. I filled out an application."

"To be *arranged?*" she yells.

"Shut up!" I hiss, darting a glance at Josh, whose shoulders have rolled forward and arm muscles bunch like he's clenching them. I can't tell if he can hear us or not, but I'm not eager for him to listen in on my desperate plot to sidestep the horrors of the dating game and be married. "Calm down. It was just an application."

"To be arranged?" she asks again, this time in a very loud whisper. "Are you *nuts?*"

"You just said that your parents are happy, Dee. They fall asleep together every night!"

"Court, Court, Court…" She knocks on the bar, raising

her voice a little. "Josh, my darling, we need two more, puh-lease! Stat!"

Josh turns around, but he doesn't even glance at Dina. He looks straight at me, and his face is full of so much disapproval and anger, it steals my breath.

"Wh—What?" I murmur. "What did I do?"

Shaking his head at me with disgust, he looks at Dina, his face devoid of any flirtation whatsoever. "Two more. Coming right up."

"Yeah. He's super weird today," says Dina, frowning at Josh's back before facing me. "Honey, listen, you're not Indian. You're American. And Americans do things a different way. They don't do well marrying strangers. They don't do well without established sexual compatibility, a full understanding of each other's disgusting eating habits, and a laundry list of shared life goals. These aren't things that Americans are comfortable learning about their partner *after* saying "I do." Americans like to know *exactly* what kind of car they're buying before they leave the lot. It's not enough that their well-intentioned auntie has assured them the car is solid."

"But—"

"No 'buts'!" she exclaims, holding up a manicured finger with a shiny, plum-colored nail. "Remember what I said about Indian couples growing into love? They *literally* do that. In some cases, they get married with next-to-zero feelings for the other person except for respect and hope." She scans my eyes. "Are you sure *you* can do that?"

I've asked myself the same question a hundred times

since I filled out the application last weekend, and that I still don't have an answer makes my heart heavy. I want this to work. So badly. I want to be saved from another minute of living my disappointing, frustrating, soul-killing single life.

"You don't understand," I lament.

"What don't I understand?"

"You have a security net, Dina. If *you* get sick of this—of flirting and one-night stands and stupid guys who never call back—you can just ask your parents to arrange you." She starts to shake her head, but I stand my ground. "Yes, you can! You have an escape hatch. You have loving parents who know you, who will do their best to find someone worthy of you, someone amazing." I pause, because—*what the fuck!*—my eyes are stinging and blurring. "I don't have that. I have to go on two hundred more bad dates. Two thousand. Hell, I might have to put up with a million jerks to try to find someone nice. Do you know what that does to a person's—"

"Nineteen-fifty."

"—heart?"

I jerk my head up and find Josh staring down at me, but for the first time since I've walked in tonight, his face isn't pissed or closed or angry. As he stares into my watery eyes, his expression softens, until it's almost tender. He takes a deep breath and lets it go.

"For the drinks," he adds. "Nineteen-fifty. Should I put it on your—"

I jump when a guy behind me yells, "Where's my girlfriend's cosmo?"

Josh flicks an annoyed glance at him. "Give me a

second, pal."

"Why? You're a bartender, right? You make drinks for a living? Cosmo! Now!" he barks.

"Stop being a dick," says Josh, shaking the metal container in his hand. He glances down at me. "Put it on your tab?"

"Sure," I say with a lackluster shrug.

Josh turns his back to me, and when he faces me again, he's holding a very full cosmo in his fingers. Before he can set it on the bar, I'm hip-checked as the drunken asshole behind me lunges for it.

"Finally!"

As I right myself, I knock his outstretched arm with my shoulder and the entire drink—a full glass of vodka, cranberry juice, lime juice, and triple sec—splashes over me like a hot-pink tsunami.

"Oh, shit!" yells the drunken guy behind me.

"Asshole!" bellows Josh.

"*I'm* the asshole? *She* knocked my drink over!"

I sit there, paralyzed and gasping, drenched in freezing cold cosmo.

"You're outta here!" says Josh, pushing off from the inside of the bar and vaulting over it to come back down on our side. Whoa. "You're fucking outta here, man!"

In my stupor, it occurs to me that I had no idea Josh could move like that.

Dina takes my arm. "Court, let's go to the bathroom."

"I'm soaked," I say as cosmo drips from my chin to my white silk blouse, which has become pretty porny, sticking to my body like a second skin.

The bouncer stationed at the front door comes to assist Josh with the drunken asshole, who's refusing to leave and demanding a fresh drink as Dina pulls me off my stool and puts her arm around my shoulders. "Come on. Let's try to dry you off."

"I'll help her."

We turn at the same time to find Josh standing behind us.

"You can't go into the ladies' room," says Dina.

"I'll take her to the employees' lounge. We have…T-shirts and stuff."

Dina looks at me. "Sound good to you, Court?"

All I want is to get out of these wet clothes, and frankly, it sounds like Josh has a better plan than paper towels or the ladies' room hand dryer.

I turn to him. "Thanks."

Pushing gently against the small of my back, he guides me toward the back of the bar, until the crowd thins out around us and he can walk beside me. Tidewaters isn't exactly a small place, and we walk through a dining room and a huge game room outfitted with pool tables before coming to a door with a card reader next to the handle. Josh swipes a card, then opens and holds the door so that I can precede him.

I step into a carpeted hallway, waiting for him to join me and lead the way. I follow him to another door, and once we're inside, he flicks on the lights. We're in a lounge/dining room area that's pretty swanky.

"This is…nice."

"Yeah," he says. "Lulu and Harvey—they're the owners—meet clients here. You know, to plan private events."

"People have private events at Tidewaters?" I've always just thought of it as an after-work watering hole.

"Yeah, sometimes," he says. I look up and realize he's staring at me—*hard*—and I cross my arms over my chest. Caught gaping, he blinks at me, clears his throat, then walks over to a closet in the corner of the room. "Umm…Lulu keeps extra T-shirts in here."

The room's walls are painted navy blue and decorated with Broadway playbills, which doesn't totally mesh with the ocean theme of the bar and grille. "Who's into Broadway?"

"Lulu," he says. "She was a chorus girl in the sixties."

I'm standing in front of a framed playbill for *Miss Saigon* when Josh comes up behind me.

"This should work," he says, his voice a little husky.

I'm aware of him. God, I'm so aware of him.

Without turning around, I ask, "Have you seen it?"

"*Miss Saigon?* Yeah."

"I loved it," I say. "It's my favorite."

"You like musicals?"

"Mm-hm. And plays."

He snorts softly, nudging my arm with the T-shirt. "I'll turn around so you can get changed."

As I peel off my blouse, I ask, "What was that scoff for?"

He pauses for a second, then asks, "What's your

favorite play?"

I throw my shirt on the floor and look over my shoulder to be sure he's turned away before unclasping my bra. "Umm. I guess…*Cyrano de Bergerac.*"

"Rostand. Huh." He sounds surprised.

"'Huh' what? Not a favorite?"

"No, it's just…you know the difference between plays and musicals. I was ready for you to say *Miss Saigon.*"

"Of course I know the difference," I say, pulling the T-shirt over my bare breasts and feeling a little salty about the way he's judging me.

"You'd be surprised how many people don't."

"Well, *I* do." I turn around, smoothing the blue T-shirt over my damp skirt. "All set."

When he pivots to face me, his face is gentle again, like it was right before I was doused in cosmo.

"You look good."

I smile, that warm feeling from last week returning in a wonderful rush. "If things don't work out at DeWitt, maybe I'll apply for a job."

"Do you really like plays?" he asks, his voice serious, like the question is important.

"Yeah, I do. A lot."

"My, um—my roommate is staging an updated version of *Romeo and Juliet* at the Mitzi Newhouse Theater. It's at—"

"—Lincoln Center," I finish for him. My mother is a big patron of the arts. "I know where it is."

"You wanna go?" he asks, his voice so soft I wonder for a second if I heard him right.

"Are you asking me out on a—?"

"Forget it," he says, running a hand through his hair and turning away from me.

"No, wait. I don't want to forget it."

At the door, he turns back around, and I let my eyes linger on him, this Adonis whom I've always thought was out of my league. He's tall and beautiful, with dark brown hair and full lips. For a split second, I imagine how those lips would feel on mine, and a thrill rips through me like lightning, its white-hot trail of fire pooling between my thighs like lava. I gasp softly, and his blue eyes visibly darken as they stare into mine.

"You want to go or what?" he rasps.

Do I want to go? Do I want to go to a play with Josh-the-brooding-bartender?

My mind races.

I know very little about him. So very little. I mean, I've seen him flirting with nearly every woman who walks into this place, including my friend and *excluding* me…until now. Where the heck is this coming from? Other questions pile on: What does he do when he's not here? Is this his dream job, and if it's not, what is? And when he looks at other women the way he's looking at me right now, do they feel as naked as I do? As vulnerable? As utterly conquered?

Yes, I do.

I *do* want to go to a play with hot Josh.

"Sure," I say.

He looks shocked at first, his eyes wide and surprised like he never thought I'd say yes. A second later, his expression morphs into annoyance, his eyebrows furrowing like he's angry with himself, like it was a mistake to ask me to go but now he's stuck.

Well, if that's how he feels about it…"We don't have to—"

"Meet me in front of the theater on Sunday."

I nod, leaning down to pick up my soiled clothing. "What time?"

"Four."

"Four o'clock. Okay." I want to smile at him, but I'm confused by everything happening between us—not to mention his expression, which is so intense, I can't. We stare at each other from across the lounge, he with his hand on the doorknob and me cradling my damp clothes in my arms.

Finally, I gesture to the T-shirt. "Thanks for the—"

"No problem," he says, our mutual trance broken.

He turns and pushes through the door, leaving me alone.

CHAPTER 4

<u>Josh</u>

I asked her out.

I fucking asked her out.

Fuck. What was I even thinking?

First rule of bartending: "Don't ask your customers out." Second rule: "If you feel like asking out a cute patron, refer to Rule #1."

The very reason the expression "shit where you eat" was created, it's just not smart to mix business and pleasure. Add to this, Lulu and Harvey have made it clear that it's strictly forbidden to "fraternize with the customers." Totally off-limits. I actually had to sign something when I was hired at Tidewaters that said I wouldn't date the customers. Be charming, listen, smile, and flirt a ton? Sure. But make an actual move? No. It's verboten.

So, what the fuck was I thinking?

And shit! I don't even know if Sammy *has* extra tickets to her Shakespeare reimagining, and even if she does, I'm not sure she's going to be thrilled that I offered one to someone she doesn't know, who isn't even in the theater business. It's hard as hell to get a venue as awesome as

Lincoln Center. Every seat is gold and can't be squandered on just anyone.

I stare at my reflection in the bus window, shaking my head at my stupid face.

What the actual fuck were you thinking?

But then I hear her voice in my head—the words she said to Dina coming back to me as easily as memorized lines:

If you get sick of this—of flirting and one-night stands and stupid guys who never call back—you can just ask your parents to arrange you…You have an escape hatch. You have loving parents who will do their best to find someone worthy of you, someone amazing. I don't have that. I have to go on two hundred more bad dates. Two thousand. Hell, I might have to put up with a million jerks to try to find someone nice. Do you know what that does to a person's heart?

I was straining to hear every word while she was speaking, especially after I gathered that she'd signed up with some bullshit "arranged marriage" service on the Internet. And although I was unaccountably furious that she'd pulled a stunt like that—*God only knows who she could end up with*—when I listened to the longing in her voice and turned around to see her eyes full of tears, my anger evaporated.

And then, when she was already feeling low, some shit-faced asswipe dumped a cocktail on her.

I get a strong mental picture of her standing in the breakroom looking like a soaked kitten, her shirt plastered over her ample chest and the sight of her nipples straining against the cold fabric making blood pump into my cock.

And there it is, folks! The reason I made such a dumb error in judgment by asking her out: *male weakness.*

Like every other hot-blooded guy on the face of creation, the sight of gorgeous tits in a wet blouse was enough to make all reason fly out the motherfucking window.

The bus stops at the intersection of Forty-Second and Tenth. I slide out of my seat and walk the three blocks to my apartment building in Hell's Kitchen.

Even though it's almost three o'clock in the morning, there are people on the sidewalks, which is still a marvel to me. Not that it's bustling, but it's *alive*, as it always is, and it reminds me why I love New York so much. In Minnetonka, your parents' pastor will call them up and tattle if you're loitering in front of the Taco Bell on Route 7 after ten o'clock on a Saturday night.

Speaking of home—if I'm at the play with Courtney, I'll miss the weekly call from my parents on Sunday afternoon. They call every Sunday, after they've returned home from services, coffee, and bible study at Bethlehem Lutheran. I take out my phone and make a note to catch them *before* they leave for church, to say a quick "hello." I don't want my mom to worry.

My parents are good people who raised three sons, two of whom stayed in Minnesota, and one of whom ventured into the wilds of New York. The two of them met in high school, and I can't remember a single morning that my dad didn't kiss my mom's cheek before leaving for work. They're like peanut butter and jelly. I can't imagine one without the other.

I can already hear Sunday's conversation in my head,

since it doesn't vary much from week to week.

Dad: *"What's on the docket for today, Son?"*

Joshua: *"Seeing a play at Lincoln Center."*

Mom: *"Oh, fer fun, honey!"*

I will not mention that Courtney is meeting me, because that will just open up a big can of worms, including questions about "her folks," whether or not she cooks, and if she is a "nice girl."

I chuckle softly as I take the brownstone stairs of my building two at a time and open the front door with a key. Two more sets of stairs and I'm at my door, which I open with another key.

Our apartment is like a shitty version of the apartment on the show *New Girl*—it has the same hardwood floors and exposed brick but is about an eighth of the size, with five people living there instead of four.

Jenna, who's trying to make it as a Broadway actress, is asleep on the couch in the living room, and there's no light coming from under the door of the room I share with my college friend, Mike, so he must be asleep. There is, however, light coming from Max and Sammy's room, so I rap on the door softly.

"Come in."

I open the door and peek in to find Sammy—my good friend, former roommate, and someone whom I dated for a split second after college—sitting up in bed with her laptop open, while her boyfriend, Max (who assists the head of lighting design at the Roundabout Theater) snores softly beside her.

"Hey, Sam."

She grins. "Just getting home?"

"Yeah."

"Good tips tonight?"

"A little under six hundred."

"Look at that! You made rent in one night!"

I only work at Tidewaters on Thursday and Friday nights and Sunday mornings, but I generally manage to bring in anywhere from $1,200 to $1,500 a week in tips alone. Unlike some of my coworkers, though, I claim the earnings and pay taxes on them. If I ever make it big, I don't want anyone looking back through my tax returns and discovering I stiffed Uncle Sam.

"Hey, listen…just wondering…do you have any tickets left for Sunday?"

"A few. Who wants to come?"

"A girl I know."

"What does she do?"

What Sam's really asking is this: How can said girl be helpful—is she a critic? A reviewer? Does she work for a Broadway director? How are you putting one of my tickets to good use?

"She's a friend. Her name's Courtney Salinger."

"Salinger." Sam's eyebrows raise. "Like—"

I shrug. "I don't know. Name's the same, though. And she's from Greenwich."

She pushes her laptop to the side and gets out of bed. Clad in underwear and a tank top, she crosses to her bureau, opens the top drawer, and takes out a ticket. As she hands it to me, she scans my face.

"A *friend*, huh?"

Fuck. She knows better. What is it about previous girlfriends that means they can read your face like a book?

"She hangs out at Tidewaters."

"Ha. Then she's off-limits, huh? That sucks." Sam grins like the Cheshire cat. "Listen, whether she's related to the venerable J.D. or not, maybe she could give me a soundbite? The surname may be enough to matter."

"Yeah. I'm sure she can do that."

"Cool," says Sam, leaning up on tiptoes to kiss my cheek before getting back in bed. She pulls her laptop back onto her lap and waves at me to go. "'Night, loverboy."

"'Night, Sammy," I say, pulling the door shut behind me.

***

At four o'clock on Sunday I'm standing in Hearst Plaza, at the corner of the Paul Milstein pool in front of Lincoln Center, and scanning the crowd for any sign of Courtney.

At work this morning, I made a very important decision: I can't date her. We can only be friends, and I need to make that clear to her. Today. As soon as possible.

While $6,000 a month may not sound like much to some people, my salary and tips from working at Tidewaters allow me to pursue my real passion, playwriting, on Mondays, Tuesdays, Wednesdays, and Saturdays. I'm one of fifty playwrights-in-residence at the New Dramatists, which is great, but I don't get any money from them. They give me a place to write, free Wi-Fi, use of the meeting spaces and practice stages to workshop my plays, and peer and alumni support. I need my bartending job to pay rent, keep my MetroCard full, and eat. I *can't* lose my job. If I lose my job, I lose my dream.

Which means I can't be sidetracked by Courtney Jane Salinger. No matter how much I might want to date her, I can't.

It was possibly *that* realization—that I actually *want* to date her—that shocked me more than anything else this morning. But maybe it shouldn't have. I mean, girls like Dina, for all their flirtation and hotness, aren't really my type. Not really. I've always had a thing for the girl-next-door. For girls exactly like Courtney: fresh-faced and blue-eyed, with big tits and a kind heart.

I've mentally practiced what I'm going to say to her this afternoon, but unfortunately, nothing prepares me for seeing those blue eyes under the spring sun when she taps me on the shoulder and I turn around to face her.

First of all, she's not dressed like "work" Courtney; gone are the stiff gabardine skirts and grandmotherly cashmere cardigans. Dressed in jeans with a white, button-down shirt open at the neck and rolled at the arms, she looks completely different. She's wearing heeled sandals, black sunglasses, and a bunch of bracelets on her wrist clinks together when she raises her hand in greeting. With her part-Marilyn Monroe, part-Kim Kardashian hourglass figure on display and her pretty smile lighting up Lincoln Center, she's stunning, and for the first time I can ever remember, her hair is down. Parted in the middle, it falls past her shoulders in honey-colored tresses. I'm weak for hair like that. It's all I can do not to reach out and wind a lock around my fist so I can pull her face to mine.

"Hey," she says.

I'm staring. Stop staring. Say something.

"H-Hi," I say. I'm still staring, but at least I get my mouth to work. "You, uh—Wow. You look different."

"I'm more casual on the weekends," she says, fixing the sunglasses on top of her head.

She's wearing little cream-colored pearl earrings, and I'm suddenly wondering what noises she makes when someone sucks on one of her ear lobes. The thought makes my cock twitch, and I consider what other noises she might make with other parts of her sweet flesh between my lips.

"Josh?" She tilts her head toward the theater entrance. "Should we go in?"

"Yeah. Sorry. Um, but wait. I have to say something first. To you."

She blinks at me. "Okay."

"This is awkward," I mutter.

"Just say it."

"This isn't a date," I blurt out, which sounds nothing like the line I'd rehearsed about how awesome she is and how any guy would be lucky to take her out.

"Oh." Her smile reverses until her lips are flatlined. "Okay."

"I don't—crap. I mean, any guy would be lucky to take you out."

"Yeah. Right."

"Tidewaters—my bosses at Tidewaters—they don't let us date the customers."

She gives me a look that reads: *"What a crock."*

"Really," I insist.

"Josh. I'm a regular. You flirt with every girl who walks in there."

I do. Except you. It's like I knew deep inside that you were my kryptonite, and I was trying to protect myself.

"It might look like that—"

"It *is* that."

"—but I swear to God, Courtney, it's just flirting. I've never dated a customer. Never even met someone outside of work until now."

Her little pink tongue darts out to lick her lips, and I swallow a groan as my cock pulses again. This would be a whole lot easier if I weren't so fucking attracted to her.

"Fine. We're not on a date. We're just two human beings sitting next to each other at a play. Okay?"

Not okay. Not feeling okay at all.

"Yeah. Thanks for understanding."

"No problem," she says, heading toward the theater doors. "I'm—I mean, I'm sort of busy anyway. *Not* dating."

"You're busy *not dating*?" I ask, following her inside the theater.

"No. Well, yes. I'm not dating anymore. Ever. It's soul-crushing." She clears her throat. "I've got plans."

Right. Your stupid arranged-by-website plan.

"Still on a quest for your husband-to-be?"

She stops and turns to look at me. "Yeah. Maybe."

"How's that going? I never asked. You left the bar last week on a hunt for marriage." I glance at her bare ring finger. "Looks like you're still hunting."

"Just because it hasn't happened yet doesn't mean it won't." She gives me a half-smile. "I've secured assistance."

"Really? In what form?"

She starts walking again and I fall into step beside her.

"If you must know, I've recruited experts to help me."

"Like a dating service?"

"Nope," she said. "You're not listening. I don't date anymore. In fact, I'm *anti*dating."

"Okay," I say, giving our tickets to the usher, who returns them along with two playbills. I don't need to look at the cover. I helped Sammy design them. "A matchmaking service?"

"Mm-hm," she hums. "Let's go with that."

"They're going to find you a husband, huh?"

"With luck," she says, looking up at me. "Where are we sitting?"

I've stopped just inside the theater. I hate everything about her dumb plan, and I especially hate the way she's making something utterly insane sound so normal.

I look down at the tickets in my hand. "G5 and G7."

"Over there. Come on."

I'm feeling pretty miserable as I follow her to our seats. What if the "experts" find her a psychopathic ax murderer? Or worse, what if they find her the man of her dreams? My eyes slip to her rounded ass encased in denim. It's lush and womanly, and I itch to grab it, to pull her up against me and grind my hard cock into her—

"Here we are," she says. "Do you want five or seven?"

I'm so grumpy, I couldn't care less. "Whatever."

She shrugs, heading into the row. "Fine. I'll take seven. You know? You're pretty moody lately."

I plop down beside her. "Is that right?"

"Yes, that is right," she says, thumbing through her program. "You're almost crotchety."

"Cantankerous?"

"Sullen."

"Querulous?"

"Irritable."

"Crabby?"

"Downright grouchy," she says, looking up at me and grinning the sweetest smile. My heart clenches.

I'm smiling back at her. I know it. Damn it.

Just friends, I remind myself, turning away, even as much as it aches to stop looking at her.

"My ex-girlfriend, Sammy, wrote this play," I say.

"Your ex, huh?"

"We went to NYU together. Dated for a couple of months after college."

"Except you told me on Friday that she's your roommate. Rooming with an ex has to be…complicated."

"It's not. We're really good friends. She and her boyfriend, Max, have one bedroom. I share mine with my buddy, Mike. Jenna's on the couch."

"Jenna?"

"Actress. Mike plays the trumpet, Max is into lighting

design, and Sammy and I are playwrights. We all share a shoebox in Hell's Kitchen."

"It sounds chic and desperate," she says, "all you artists living together in squalor."

"No charge for the squalor."

"Like something out of *La Bohème*."

"Or *Rent*," I say.

She nods at me with that sweet grin. "As I said."

…which means she knows that *Rent* is a reboot of *La Bohème,* which I find so fucking sexy I have to cover my crotch with my playbill, so she doesn't see my pants tenting.

Fuck, but this sucks.

She's fresh-faced and gorgeous, knows her plays, musicals, and—apparently—operas, can bandy words with ease, is a loyal friend to Dina, a great tipper to me, and lately, she makes my heart flip-flop like I'm a teenager again.

As the lights go down and she shifts in her seat beside me, I'm barely aware of the Capulets and Montagues slinging insults on stage. All I can think about is the fact that Courtney Jane Salinger is going to find a husband sooner rather than later, and there's simply no way that lucky guy can be me.

CHAPTER 5

All things considered, it was a good show.

I liked it.

I liked the way Juliet's sensibilities were written into Romeo's character and Romeo's plotline was given to his ladylove. You'd think it wouldn't work, but by and large, it did. And the ending was depressing as hell, just as it should be.

Speaking of depressing, Josh tossing me into the friendzone the second I arrived at the theater rated high on a scale from one to Depressing. Not that I should be surprised. I know what I look like: I'm a solid and confident 7, but Josh is an 11.

Not that it matters. Because I really don't *want* to date Josh. That's not my plan. I don't want to date anyone anymore.

I guess I never expected him to ask me out, and when he did, I gave myself permission to see him in a new way. I gave myself permission to be attracted to him. And I guess I just didn't expect to feel this much chemistry with him. *One-sided* chemistry, because he couldn't have made it more clear that he's not interested in dating me. I don't know. Maybe

I'm a little embarrassed. Or maybe I liked feeling attractive to someone as insanely hot as Josh. Or maybe, for a millisecond, I envisioned dating him, and, just for that millisecond, I liked the way it looked.

But whatever.

It's for the best, I tell myself. *You've got a whole new life around the corner, and it doesn't include Josh.*

I smile at the doorman as I step outside the theater.

After the show, Josh said he needed to go backstage to congratulate his "friend," Sammy, and I said I'd wait for him outside. Now that I'm standing here alone, though, I'm feeling silly and borderline pathetic. He probably wants to hang out with his friends, right? Celebrate the fact that one of them just staged a production at Lincoln Center?

Taking a deep breath, I push away from the cement column behind me and start walking toward the iconic Josie Robertson Plaza with its gorgeous fountain. A musician from Juilliard has pushed a grand piano into the plaza, and he's playing a plaintive melody that perfectly echoes my mood.

Pausing, I dig through my purse for a coin to throw into the fountain, but when I close my eyes to make a wish, my mind goes blank. A light breeze, more summer than spring, blows my hair against my cheek, and I feel my eyes well with tears behind my lids. There is no city more completely *alive* than New York City, and yet I'm standing here alone. How I wish I had someone to share it with.

I open my eyes and let the coin roll into the fountain.

As the music swells to a dramatic crescendo, I hear a

husky voice close to my ear.

"What did you wish for?"

"I…" I turn around to find a smiling Josh standing close to me. Even with my heels on, he's several inches taller than I am, and I have to tilt my head back a little to look into his eyes. "If I tell, it won't come true."

"Hey." His eyes scan my face and his eyebrows furrow. "You're sad."

I lift my chin. "I'm fine."

"What happened?"

I'm not about to tell him—this man who has zero romantic interest in me whatsoever—that I long for a *someone* so desperately that sometimes it makes me want to cry.

"*Romeo and Juliet* isn't exactly cheerful," I say, because it's easier and self-preserving.

"Nor is Rachmaninoff," he says, scowling at the pianist.

"Is that what this is?"

He nods. "It's called *Rhapsody on a Theme of Paganini*."

"It's pretty."

"But melancholy."

He sits down on the wall of the fountain, and I sit down beside him, watching as a small crowd of people claps for the pianist, who launches into another classical piece I don't recognize.

"You didn't have to leave your friends," I say. "I was going to slip away."

"Why? You said you'd wait for me."

"You should go back," I say, but he doesn't. He stays where he is, sitting beside me as another warm breeze makes my hair tickle my cheek. But this time, my eyes don't well with tears.

"What did you think?" he asks. "Of the play?"

"Good."

"Yeah," he says. "But not great."

"Solidly good," I insist.

He nudges me with his elbow. "But not great."

"But not great," I agree.

"I have been watching her workshop this idea for five years. Maybe longer. And I know that as a concept, it's good. 'Flip Romeo and Juliet on its ear with a gender swap!' It's easy to market, easy to sell, and yet…" He huffs out a frustrated breath. "Yet, it's not going anywhere, and it's not going to. It's just not…quite…good…*enough*."

His voice is rough and filled with discouragement. I want to comfort him, but I'm not sure what to say.

He sighs. "You could write a play that was in the top half percent of all the plays written in the whole world—in the whole span of artistic mankind—but if it's not in the top *point two* percent, it won't go anywhere."

"Point two percent can change the world," I say.

"Unfortunately," he mutters.

"Tell that to the paraplegic who has a point two percent chance of walking again."

Silence settles between us while the pianist continues playing.

Finally, I ask, "Do you know what I do? For a living?"

"You work at a brokerage firm, right?"

"At a hedge fund. I work in quantitative analytics."

"You're *literally* speaking Greek to me. I have no idea what any of that means. Hedge funds make me think of shrubbery."

I grin at that. "I predict outcomes that investors use in their decision-making."

"Are you usually right?"

I nod. "I have a brain for numbers. Statistics. Probability. Always have."

"So, cut to the chase. What does that have to do with Sammy's play?"

I cross my arms over my chest and shake my head. "It's a no-go."

"Fuck," he mutters. "I mean, I knew that. I *know* that. I just…"

"You want your ex-girlfriend to succeed."

He turns and looks at me. I can feel the heat of his eyes, though I don't meet them. Finally, he exhales the breath he's been holding, and it sounds frustrated.

"She's *just* my friend. I don't even know why I told you we dated. It was a hundred years ago. It's irrelevant."

"Tell me about your play," I say to change the subject. Whoever she is to Josh, it doesn't feel good to hear about her.

"I have two that I've been workshopping at the New Dramatists for a couple of years: *Miss Gibson Will See You Now* and *Catching Caufield*."

"Caufield. Is that a *Catcher in the Rye* reference?"

"It is," he says. "So, I *have* to ask—"

"No relation," I say.

"You've been asked that all your life, haven't you?"

"Uh-huh," I say, grinning at a mother and daughter dressed in their Sunday best and taking a selfie by the fountain.

"You're sure he's not a long-lost uncle or something?"

"My father was an only child."

"That settles it then. How about you? Only child, like your dad?"

"Yes, actually."

"I'm one of three," he offers, "and my parents are each one of six."

"Whoa! Big family," I say, looking up at him.

"Small family," he answers, looking down at me.

The lights of the fountain are reflected in his eyes, even more now that dusk is falling around us. They look like a universe marked with a million sparkling stars, and I'm lost in them as I keep my eyes locked with his. The pianist launches into a whole new piece of music, and it pierces my soul as he plays.

"What is this?"

"Debussy. *Clair de Lune*." Josh swallows, his eyes still fixed on mine. "Why didn't I meet you at a different time?"

He leans his head closer to mine, and when our foreheads touch, I close my eyes.

"When?"

"When I had a hit. When I was successful. When I could…*do* this." His hand reaches up to cup my jaw, and I open my eyes to find his, intense and beseeching. "Do you understand? It's all I've worked for. It's my dream. It's what

I want more than anything else. I have to stay focused. You get that, don't you?"

Clair de Lune continues, chords following one after the other, roiling and intense. They somehow echo the wild aching of my heart as my own dreams fill my head:

I want a house in suburbia with a white picket fence.

I want babies to buckle into a minivan.

But most of all, I want a husband.

I want to be married.

I want to share all this goodness with someone I love, with someone who loves me back.

I can barely fill my lungs, but I reach up and cover his hand, gently removing it. "I do, Josh-the-playwright. I understand."

I reach for my purse, then hop off the wall, facing him.

"Thanks for inviting me tonight," I say.

His gaze is intense, but inscrutable. "Courtney—"

"Good night," I say, turning around and hurrying down the steps to Columbus Avenue, where a line of cabs awaits.

I don't look back.

And Josh lets me go.

***

Twenty minutes later, I'm home.

Shoes off, sweats on, fake fireplace throwing off real heat, and takeout on its way as I open my laptop and check my e-mail.

As my computer connects to the building's Wi-Fi, I think about what Josh said:

Why didn't I meet you at a different time?

My heart clutches a little.

I'd just convinced myself that he wasn't attracted to me and made peace with it. And now? Now it seems I was wrong. After that moment at the fountain, against all odds, our attraction to each other is undeniable.

Isn't it funny how life is sometimes? Funny terrible, not funny ha-ha.

For the last year or so, I thought Josh was into Dina, and I didn't allow myself to see him as anything but my Friday evening pal, Josh-the-bartender. And then one night, out of nowhere, clarity is offered, and everything changes: he's not into Dina, and she's not into him. The floodgates open. And everything you never knew you were keeping dammed-up bursts forth.

How long have I been quietly mooning over him? Always? And how long has he been attracted to me?

I can still remember last May, when I walked into Tidewaters on a Friday night to find a "new guy" behind the bar. Scanning his tall, muscled body and tousled dark hair, I remember thinking he was hot. Like every other girl in the bar, I was attracted him. But at some point, or over time, I stopped seeing him as eye candy and started looking forward to his friendly smile, to his funny observations, and sometimes, when it was a quiet night, to our long conversations.

A different time?

We had a year to *see* each other but never really did. And now that we have? The timing's all wrong.

"I quit. I quit. I quit," I mutter, remembering everything

I hate about dating: one-night stands, booty calls, guys who don't call back, mixed messages—and now? Bad timing.

"God, my luck is shit."

I click on my e-mail icon and the program opens. When I click on "New Messages," a subject line immediately catches my eye:

"YOU'VE BEEN CHOSEN TO BE ARRANGED"

All thoughts of Josh fly out the window, and I lean forward as my heart starts galloping. I click on the e-mail.

Dear Ms. Salinger:

Thank you for filling out our application with honesty and care.

We can tell that you are someone who is earnestly seeking a forever match, and we are excited to find that special someone for you, Courtney Jane Salinger.

It generally takes four to six weeks for us to match your profile to that of someone in our growing database. Why so long? Because we take every match seriously, and choose each and every ArrangeMeToo.com partnership with discrimination, integrity, and diligence.

Were we to rush the process of finding your perfect mate, we wouldn't maintain the 90 percent satisfaction rate we presently hold with our clients.

While you are waiting for us to contact you with the e-mail address of your future spouse, we encourage you to ready your mind and heart for a married-at-first-sight match. How?

1. Nurture an optimistic heart. No endeavor will be successful unless it has 100 percent of your hope, faith and optimism. Open your heart to the person we choose for you, so that you can move forward into your marriage with a positive, can-do attitude.

2. Prepare yourself for marriage. When you're ready (there's no time like the present!) stop dating. Some of our brides-to-be buy an engagement ring and wear it as a reminder that a new life is imminent. Start thinking of yourself as half of a partnership, and it will make it easier for you once you actually are.

3. Place a premium on friendship. Many of our couples find that attraction isn't instantaneous and must be cultivated. One of the best ways to do this? By becoming friends first. Find out what you have in common and how to align your goals. If a solid and caring friendship develops, love will often follow.

4. Be clear about your expectations. Will it bother you if he goes out with male friends every Saturday and leaves you at home? Be up front. Likewise, if you expect him to join you for dinner at your parents' once a week, tell him how much this means to you. Don't expect him to figure you out. Meet him halfway.

5. Take your time. The most wonderful thing about being married at first sight is that you have the rest of your life together to fall in love. Not initially attracted? No problem. Let love (and attraction!) grow. Learn how to love your partner and teach him how to love you back. To make this happen, patience is key.

When we have determined your match, we will

contact you (and your future spouse) together in one e-mail. We will explain why we feel you have the potential to have a lasting and loving marriage, and we will encourage you to trade a few e-mails to decide where and when your wedding will take place.

Please note that our sister website, ArrangeMyWedding.com, can help you with any specific wedding-day details, and you are even entitled to a 10 percent discount for using our matchmaking service. Should you require marriage counseling in the early days of your union, we are pleased to offer hourly rates for our personalized in-person and Skype services. It is important to us that you feel 100 percent supported on your chosen path!

We are so excited for you to begin your journey and expect to share your match with you on approximately June 1.

Until then, feel free to reach out to us with any questions, Courtney Jane Salinger, and work on preparing your heart and mind to meet the love of your life.

With affection,

Dr. Jake, Pastor Ken, and Dr. Sydney Morningstar.
Your ArrangeMeToo.com Team

I read the e-mail once and then go back and read it twice more, concentrating on the five list items and stopping each time to stare at the date, June 1, when I will finally be placed in contact with my future husband.

It's scary, but also spectacular, to think that the wheels on this deal are already moving. I highlight the list and print it out, pinning it to the corkboard in my kitchen and rereading the tips again. I mean to take them seriously—to do everything I can to be in the right mind-set for my arranged marriage when June 1 finally rolls around.

And now that I've received and read this e-mail? Part of me is grateful Josh was so clear that we weren't actually on a date tonight, because it makes me feel like I didn't cheat on the Arrange Me Too process.

Despite my attraction to him, I'll force myself to shift gears right away. Besides, being friends with Josh could be a great thing, seen in the right light—it would give me practice time before June. I don't have a lot of male friends, and maybe Josh would be willing to sit next to me at another show or two—just so I can hone my friendship-building skills before I meet my future husband.

To celebrate my intentions, I log on to Amazon.com and search the words "engagement ring." I don't want something expensive, but it shouldn't turn green the first time I wash my hands either. I settle on a simple, sterling silver band with a single garnet (my birth stone) and have it sent to my office.

"This is happening," I whisper to myself with a hint of awe, just as my phone rings. I pick it up to see who's calling, then grimace when the word "Mother" pops up on the screen.

"Hello," I say, pressing the phone to my ear.

"Darling! It's been ages! How are you?"

It hasn't been ages. It's been a couple of weeks since we've spoken. Three max, which is normal. It's not like we talk every day, or even every week. My parents made it clear to me from a very early age that they are very busy, very important people, and having a child wouldn't change that.

"I'm well," I say. "And you?"

"Quite well. Wasn't the weather glorious today?"

"It's certainly getting warmer."

"We were at the Drury's for lunch and had drinks alfresco on the patio. In April!"

"What a treat."

"How's work? Going well?"

"Mm-hm. Very well."

"Another few years and you may be up for partner."

"That's the plan," I say.

"Darling, I'm calling because the Fredericks have two extra seats at their daughter's wedding next Saturday, and Simi wondered if you'd like to come."

This isn't as unusual as it sounds.

Rich Connecticut types who have already paid their country club catering for so many meals can't bear to have some of it go to waste due to last-minute cancellations, so they'll invite their friends' single children to attend the event and fill the empty seats. Matchmaking is often a secondary goal of such an invitation, however, so I'm immediately wary. *When you're ready, stop dating.*

"Darling? Are you free?"

"Who is the second seat for?"

"What do you mean?"

"You said that the Fredericks have two extra seats. If I'm taking one, who's taking the other?"

"That's the best part! Have you met their nephew, Brant? Brant Summerfield? He can sit next to you, and they'll shuffle Reginald's aunt to another other table."

"Mother, you know how I feel about blind dates."

"Darling, he's a catch, I promise. Plus, you'd be doing Simi such a favor. Please say you'll come. We haven't seen you since Easter."

I'm overdue to visit, and I'd like to see my parents, but I can't agree to a date. It wouldn't be right.

Suddenly, I think of Josh. He has no interest in dating me, but if he'd go with me, as an escort and nothing more, I could (1) please my mother by attending, (2) sidestep a blind date with Brant Summerfield, and (3) maintain a clear conscience, since I wouldn't actually be on a date.

"May I bring my own escort?"

"My dear! I had no idea you were attached to someone! Of course. Do we know him?"

"No. He's a playwright."

"Oh, darling," she says, her cultured voice lowering with disappointment. "Tsk."

"It's casual," I say.

"If it's so casual, then come and meet Brant instead."

"No, thank you."

"Very well. You know I'm the staunchest supporter of the arts. Does he have a tux?"

"I've no idea."

"Well, you can sort that with him, I suppose. His

69

name?"

"Josh Dalton."

"Dalton. That's promising! Of the New York Daltons?"

I grin. *No charge for the squalor.* I doubt very much he has a trust fund if his bartending income is so important and he lives in a Hell's Kitchen hovel.

"No."

"Boston?"

"I don't think so."

"Philadelphia?"

"Mother." It occurs to me that I have no idea where Josh is from. In all the times we've chatted, I've never asked, which makes me feel a bit ashamed. "We'll see you on Saturday."

"Go directly to Riverside Yacht Club from the train, darling," she says. "See you there at six."

"Six it is."

"How lovely. Don't forget your girdle, darling."

For the love of God. "Good-bye, Mother."

I press "End" on my phone and place it on the table.

Tomorrow I'll track down Josh to see if he'll be my date—er, um, *escort*—to Hope Frederick's Greenwich wedding. Fingers crossed he's willing and able, because his disinterest in dating me has suddenly made him the safest man I can think of.

Then, with that settled in my mind, I open my e-mail again and reread the instructions from my Arrange Me Too experts over and over again until my dinner arrives.

CHAPTER 6

Josh

"Call for you."

I look up from rewrites to find the receptionist standing in the doorway of the studio where I've been writing all afternoon. "Huh?"

"Phone call."

Phone call?

During my five years in residence at the New Dramatists, I can't remember someone calling for me. Anyone who wants to talk to me has my cell phone number. *Unless…*

My heart lurches.

…it's someone who's heard about one of my plays!

I jump up from my desk so fast the chair crashes back on the floor, but I ignore it as I hustle to the front office. I've heard of stuff like this. *The Call.* Someone who's gotten wind of your play, your concept, your name—the friend of a friend of a college professor, or the co-worker's sister's uncle who happens to be a producer looking for new blood.

I get to the office, and just for a minute, I stare at the phone sitting on the receptionist's desk with the red "Hold" button blinking slowly.

Could this be it? The often-dreamed-of "before" moment, after which my entire life changes?

I clear my throat, pick up the receiver, and press it to my ear.

"Hello? This is Josh Dalton."

"Hi. It's Courtney."

I blink.

"Who?"

"Courtney," she says. "Courtney Salinger? From Tidewaters? From yesterday—"

"I know who you are," I say.

"Oh. Okay. Um, well, I hope I'm not bothering you, but I had a favor to ask."

"Why are you calling me here?"

I don't mean to be rude or abrupt, and honestly, there is a part of me that's glad to hear her voice. But *most* of me wants to punish her a little for inadvertently getting my hopes up so high.

"Sorry."

The small sound of her voice makes me feel bad. "It's okay. Sorry for the attitude—I just, um…I've never gotten a call here before. I thought that maybe…"

"Oh, my God! You thought I was calling about your play."

"Context is everything. When I'm *here*…"

"…you're a playwright! God, I'm *so* sorry, Josh. I didn't mean to do that to you."

I lean against the wall of the small office, a smile teasing at the corners of my mouth. I can see her face in my head so clearly—her sweet, apple cheeks and lush, pink lips—as she apologizes so earnestly. Where is she right now? At work? In another one of those white silk blouses, wearing little pearl earrings that tempt me to lap the skin around them?

"It's okay. What's up? Everything okay?"

"Yeah. Everything's fine." She pauses. "I feel like an idiot now."

"Nah. It's okay." The receptionist returns to her desk with a cup of coffee and gives me a look pronouncing this space her domain. "Listen, can I call you back in two minutes?"

We swap numbers and I return to the studio I'm using today, closing the door before dialing her number.

"Hi, again," I say, easing into my chair and putting my feet up on the desk. "How's it going?"

"Okay for a Monday," she says, then adds, "Did you know that twenty percent of heart attacks happens on Mondays?"

"Cheery."

"And sixteen percent of suicides."

I laugh. "Wow. Thanks for calling to tell me that."

"I'm nervous," she says. "I don't call guys very often."

"No?"

"No." She pauses, and I can almost hear her gulping as she gets to the point of her call. "But we're friends, aren't we? And friends can call each other."

"Sure," I say. "We're friends."

…if your definition of "friends" is two people of the opposite sex

who are clearly attracted to each other, and but for better circumstances would have woken up next to one another this morning. Sure. We're friends. Let's go with that.

"Phew. I thought so, but I needed to make sure." I'm about to ask why when she continues: "I need an escort to a wedding on Saturday night, but obviously I can't bring a date."

"Obviously?"

"The matchmakers?" she reminds me.

I flinch, taking a deep breath and letting it go in a long-suffering huff. "I've been meaning to ask: Are you sure that's a good idea?"

"What?"

"Your *matchmaker* service?"

"Yes," she answers. "It's an excellent idea. It's working."

My feet hit the ground as I sit up straight. "You've been matched?"

"No!" She chuckles softly. "Not yet. But I've been accepted into the program. I'll meet my husb—um, my *match*, by June 1."

You were about to say "husband," I think, every muscle in my body bunching with resistance at the thought.

"That's soon," I grind out.

"Yes." She clears her throat. "Anyway, they advise that I should stop dating other people now. You know—so I can prepare myself to meet the guy they choose for me. But my parents want me to go to the wedding of one of their friends' daughters. If I show up alone, they'll try to set me up, so I need an escort. Someone who understands—"

"That you're not actually available."

"Exactly! I knew you'd understand."

"When is it?"

"Saturday night in Greenwich. We could meet at Grand Central at five o'clock and take the train out together. You're invited to stay overnight at my parents' house, as well."

"I have to work on Sunday morning."

"Then my parents' driver can drop you back at the station on Saturday night."

Parents' driver? "What kind of wedding is this?"

"Have you heard of the Fredericks? Samantha and Reginald Frederick? Samantha, whom we call Simi, is my mother's best friend."

Samantha and Reginald Frederick? Fuck, yes, I've heard of them. Anyone who watches PBS's *Masterpiece Theater* has heard of them. They're the people thanked for "their generous donation" *by name* just before each new episode airs.

"I've heard of them."

"Do you have a tux?"

Actually, I do. It's a good investment when you are occasionally invited to Broadway and off-Broadway premieres and want to be taken seriously.

"Yes."

"Great! So, you'll do it? You'll come with me?"

"Sure."

"Meet me at the clock at Grand Central on Saturday? Five o'clock?"

"I'll be there," I say.

"Thanks, Josh," she says softly. "Bye."

"Bye."

I place my phone on the desk and lean back in the chair again, staring up at the ceiling.

This girl. With her weirdo statistics and hot body, her blind trust in this marriage service and the way she underplays a connection like the Fredericks. She is so fascinating to me, if I don't watch it, I'm going to fall for her…which is definitely not allowed.

I sit up and open my laptop, glancing at the scene I was tweaking before I impulsively click on Chrome. The search bar comes up, and I type in the name I'd overheard he mention to Dina at the bar: "arrange me too matchmaking." A second later, a glossy website comes up with pictures of happy couples and three smiling "experts."

I groan, shaking my head. "What a load of shit."

I spend half an hour checking out the website, rolling my eyes at the "testimonials" (which sound canned to me) and scoffing loudly when I note the "processing fee." Four hundred dollars is a small fortune to someone like me, but frankly, it doesn't feel like enough for a top-notch matchmaking service, which is confirmed by a quick web search that finds a high-end Manhattan matchmaker charging $10,000 for a six-month contract. And I really don't like it that all they actually promise to deliver is an e-mail address. *Four hundred beans* for an e-mail address? As far as I'm concerned, this has "scam" written all over it. How come someone as smart as Courtney can't see that?

I have to go on two hundred more bad dates. Two thousand. Hell, I might have to put up with a million jerks to try to find someone nice. Do you know what that does to a person's heart?

She laid it all out for me the first night we talked about it. She's sick of the dating game. She's confused by it. She's disheartened. She's desperate enough to sign up for a service that will give her some random guy's e-mail address with the promise that he's "the one."

And what about *that* guy?

How will she know if his intentions are good? How will she know if he's a decent person, let alone the right person for her? She's got so much riding on this, so much blind faith in the process, they could sell her just about anyone, and she'd try to make it work.

She could get hurt.

Badly.

I slam my laptop shut.

"Not my problem," I say aloud. "Not my problem and I'm not *making* it my problem."

We're friends, aren't we?

I grimace, tenting my hands on the desk and resting my chin on them. Would I let Sammy willfully do something like this without trying to warn her off? Would I stand by and watch *her* make a huge mistake and say nothing?

No way. I wouldn't let any of my friends walk into a shitstorm without at least a warning first.

If Courtney and I are going to be friends, I have a responsibility to try to talk her out of this, or at least open her eyes to the dangers of the situation. It has nothing to do with the fact that, given different circumstances, she'd be at the top of the list of women I'd like to date. It's just about doing the right thing.

I'll talk to her this weekend, I tell myself, then reopen my laptop and try to get back to work. It's futile. Hurricane Courtney has already ripped through my quiet afternoon and left my concentration in shreds.

***

Standing at the iconic clock in the middle of Grand Central Station, I scan the Vanderbilt staircase for Courtney.

I saw her briefly last night at the bar, but she was with a bunch of people from work who had a big table in the back. As she left, she stopped by the bar and reminded me about meeting her this evening, but that was the extent of our conversation.

As if I could have forgotten our nondate date.

I wrenched my neck last night while straining for a glimpse of her from my station at the bar. I could barely think about anything except the fact that she was near; disappointed that she wasn't keeping me company at the bar, I was still glad just to know she was around.

And now here I am, dressed in my secondhand tux, standing by a gold clock, and waiting for her to arrive. Any onlooker would think it romantic. Any onlooker would be wrong.

I tell myself I shouldn't feel slighted that Courtney asked me to be her escort, not her date. Hell, it's my doing. I friend-zoned her first, after all. I can't do that to her and then be a dick about it. I'll take responsibility for my actions and be a friend to her. It's the least I can do, right?

I just wish that "friends" was how I felt about her.

I mean, I want to be her friend. I do.

But every time I'm near her, there's this increasingly unavoidable feeling I want more of.

No, I don't need distractions from playwriting.

No, I don't want to lose my paying job.

I just wish there was a way to have it all.

Just as quickly as that thought arrives, it departs…and my mind goes utterly blank.

Because the *only* thing I can see—the *only* thing I can think about—is the way Courtney Jane Salinger looks walking down those marble stairs to meet me.

Under a light, beige trench coat, which sails behind her with every graceful step she takes, she wears a floor-length, gold-sequined dress that dips into a low V between her breasts and hugs every luscious curve of her body. There's a high slit up one side of the skirt that flashes peekaboo glimpses of her creamy upper thigh as she descends, and on her feet are silver sling-back heels that sparkle as she moves and frame two neat rows of fire-engine red toenails.

Every man in the station is pausing to admire her, to wonder about her, to wish—for one fucking second of our mostly Neanderthal lives—that she belonged to them.

So, when she smiles at me and lifts her hand to wave hello—to claim *me,* over and in spite of every other man present—it makes goosebumps rise on my arms. More than half my blood sluices to my groin, where it pools, pressure building with every pulse. It's lust. It's desire. It's the insistent and age-old hunger of a man to fuck his woman. And yeah, it's been watered down by centuries of rules and manners, but it's loud and strong and screams to me that it's still there, throbbing and alive, deep inside of me.

She is a goddess. A princess. A queen.

I'm a mere mortal, undeserving of someone like her, but it doesn't matter. I fucking want her anyway. And now that I've admitted it to myself, there's no way I'll ever be able to deny it again.

I raise my hand in answer to hers and step away from the clock to walk toward her. I long to kiss her on the cheek, and if this were any other woman, I would. But I'm losing my boundaries and my senses where Courtney is concerned. I'm not certain I could stop once I started, and since we've firmly decided that we're not interested in pursuing more than friendship with each other, it's just not a good idea to touch her at all.

I put my hands in my pockets. "Hey."

"Hi," she says, her smile broadening as she gets closer. "Sorry I'm late!"

Guileless and totally lovely.

"Can I ask you something?"

"Sure," she says.

"Do you *not* notice the way every guy in this station is staring at you?"

She blinks at me, then looks around us for a second before catching my eyes again. "I'm overdressed for Grand Central."

"No, Courtney. It's not because you're overdressed. It's

because you're stunning."

She laughs at me. "Don't be silly." Her swanlike neck twists so that she can look up at the posted tracks and train times. She points to an express train headed to New Haven that stops at Greenwich. "Upper Level. Track 24. Come on."

We find two seats facing each other on the train. She chooses a window seat, and I do the same.

"Thanks so much for doing this," she says, shrugging off her coat. "It shouldn't be too painful. Drinks. Dinner. Dancing. A few toasts. No big deal."

She's right: the party's no big deal. What *is* a big deal is the way she looks in this dress. With her honey hair piled on her head in a complicated braided style and ruby-red lipstick on her lips, she looks delicious.

"Will you know a lot of people?" I ask, forcing myself to make polite conversation.

"Probably. And my parents will be there, of course."

"Who am I to you?" I ask. Her eyes widen for a second and her lips part like she's trying to figure out what to say. It takes me a second to realize that she's misunderstanding me. "Just so I know what to say in case anyone asks."

"Oh! Oh, right. Um. My escort," she says. "A friend."

I nod slowly, because my thoughts since the moment I saw her tonight haven't even been in the same area code as "friendly."

More people enter the train, and she takes out her phone, looking at messages and typing out a response to at least one before slipping her phone back into her purse. Meanwhile, I try to figure out a way to back into a conversation about how using a scam matchmaking service might not be the best way to find a spouse.

"Can I talk to you about something?" I ask her.

She nods. "Sure."

"Remember that night at the bar? A couple of weeks ago? The night you left in search of marriage?"

"Yes."

"You said something that stuck with me. You said that everyone's playing games, but it's not fun. You said that you were sick and tired of dating. You said you just wanted the real thing."

"That's all true."

"So, here's the thing: I don't understand why you're single. I feel like you should be able to meet someone organically."

She stares back at me for a moment before offering a polite smile. "Are you serious?"

"Yeah, I am. You're beautiful. You're smart. You're funny. You're kind. You have a good job. You have your own apartment. I have a fair idea that you're loaded. Why has it been so hard for you?"

As I speak, I watch her face—the way her polite smile disappears, the way her eyebrows delicately furrow as I talk about her, and finally, the way she drops my gaze altogether, staring down at her clasped hands.

"Courtney?"

"Are you making fun of me?" Her voice is barely a whisper.

"What? No!"

She looks up at me, and when she does, her eyes are glassy. "You mean it?"

I recoil, shocked by her question. "Yeah. Of course."

"You think I'm beautiful, smart, funny, and kind?" Her voice is so heart-breakingly full of hope, it claws at my own heart. *Would that I could offer you more than friendship, sweet woman.*

"I wouldn't have said so if I didn't." And then, because I perceive that my heart's going to beat right out of my chest, I neutralize the comment as best I can, putting myself back in check. "I expect a lot from my friends, Courtney. I wouldn't want to hang out with you if I didn't think you were awesome."

Her expression sobers, closing up just a little—just enough.

"I'm not beautiful. I'm just attractive," she says. "I mean, I made an effort tonight, but I'm not *usually* beautiful, and I certainly don't make an effort to be. I work with almost all men. I wear plain clothes and plain sweaters, my hair in a bun, and almost no makeup, because I want to be taken seriously."

She's ridiculous if she thinks that her natural beauty doesn't shine through her frumpy clothes, and I'm about to say so when she continues.

"I *am* smart, but that can intimidate people, you know, if you don't hide it a little." She laughs ruefully. "Not every guy would've been as generous as you were when I shared those Monday suicide statistics."

"I thought it was amusing," I say, then rush to add:

"Not that people commit suicide on Mondays, but that you had Monday facts to pull out of thin air."

"There's a delicate line between funny and weird."

"You're not weird," I assure her.

She shrugs. "Sometimes I am."

"Fine. We all are. I like a little weird in my friends too."

She grins, but this time, it's not a half-smile. It's genuine, and part of me wishes I could bask in its warmth forever.

"As for kind…" she begins.

I hold up a hand, stopping her. "I've watched you with Dina for over a year. No matter who she talks to, how late she arrives or wants to stay or who she abandons you to flirt with—you stay, you wait, you return. You buy two times the number of drinks that she does, and you never ask her for a cent. And you *always* make sure she's in a cab or has cab fare at the end of the night. You're a good friend, Courtney. Through and through."

"Or maybe I'm a little bit of a chump," she says, her eyes wistful as she stares into mine.

"How so?"

"Maybe sometimes," she begins cautiously, "it's easier to be kinder to others than myself." There is a long pause between us until she breaks it. "Josh?"

I'm frustrated with her but work to keep my voice level.

"I say you're beautiful, and you say you're plain. I say you're smart, and you say you're intimidating. I say you're funny, and you say you're weird. I say you're kind, and you say you're a chump," I tell her. "I can't tell you all the things that are good about you without you refusing to accept them. Why can't I be right?"

"Inside of me," she says softly, "I'm overwhelmed that you think so well of me. Believe me, Josh, I will hold onto those words for a long, long time. They'll give me courage to do things I never knew I could do. I will consider them and cherish them, and more than anything else, I'll hope you're right about me."

"I *am* right," I tell her.

"Shades of blue," she says, gently dismissing my point of view—or elevating her own—by saying that who she is, rather than fact, is more a matter of point of view.

Except I'm right about her. I know I am. That she is beautiful, smart, funny and kind are facts and not up for dispute, no matter how hard she is on herself.

"I forgot to add something," I say, reaching for her hand and taking it gently in mine. It's soft and warm and so much smaller than mine. "You're self-aware. You're blisteringly and brutally self-aware. You *see* yourself, but...but...in all the wrong ways. I wish you could see yourself how *I* see you, Courtney Jane Salinger. I wish you could see how wonderful you are."

She blinks rapidly, shifting slightly to face the widow. As she does, she squeezes my hand, and to my surprise, she doesn't withdraw hers.

And that's how we arrive in Greenwich forty-five minutes later: each gazing out our window, with her hand cradled tenderly in mine.

CHAPTER 7

<u>Courtney</u>

I should have known that my parents would love Josh at first sight, but I wasn't totally prepared for how my mother would fawn over him. Sitting beside my father at our assigned table, I watch Josh and my mother on the dance floor. She giggles when he spins her around, simpering like a teenager when he winks at her and pulls her back into his arms.

All those hours bartending sure did school him on how to be charming. Or maybe he was always like this?

"Penny for your thoughts, CJ."

My father wanted a son. I have known this for as long as I can remember, but I am always reminded of it when he calls me "CJ."

"Mother looks well."

"She likes your boyfriend."

"He's not my boyfriend, sir."

"Friend. Escort. Whatever he is."

"Friend will do," I say, feeling a twinge of guilt when I think of how nice my hand felt in his on the train. I can't remember the last time someone gave me such a beautiful, heartfelt compliment, and although the traits on which Josh praised me aren't the qualities on which my parents place a premium (save the smarts), it still meant a lot to me to listen to his voice, to hear his praise, and to know that he likes me on a human level, if not a romantic one.

"Can't say I approve of this artsy-fartsy stuff. He went to NYU. Solid school. Time to make something of himself."

"He is. He's working on two plays right now."

"Plays," scoffs my father. "Waste of time."

"I disagree." I've never read a word he's written, but I say, "He's talented."

"Talented or not, better he stays a—a 'friend.' You don't look out, he'll seduce you, and you'll be stuck with some freeloader working on his—his *play* for the rest of his life while you bring home the bacon."

"He's not a freeloader," I say, trying to keep my voice calm. "He earns a living."

"Doing what? Writing plays? I doubt it."

"Bartending."

"Say what, now?"

I can't let my father put down Josh. I won't.

"He's a hard worker. He bartends several times a week to finance his playwriting."

"Oh, ho! So, when he's not wasting his time dabbling with plays, he's slinging drinks? My goodness, he's a real winner, CJ. Well done."

"Will you excuse me?" I ask, because if I don't get up and leave now, I may end up saying something I regret.

"Smooth your feathers," says my father, reaching for

my wrist to keep me at the table. "We'll say no more of him."

"Thank you," I say, resettling myself in my seat.

"How's the job? What's Joel Morris got you working on, eh?"

"I'm developing a comprehensive suite of models for capital management."

"Stress testing, economic capital, and risk-adjusted return on capital?"

"All the above," I answer, taking another, bigger, sip of wine.

"And what's this I hear about a London office?"

"Should be operational by the end of May."

"Planning to go over?"

"Nothing's been offered."

"Then you should ask. My sister, Lucy, still owns the flat in London. She'd be glad to put you up for a few weeks."

I'm not going anywhere, of course, with my match coming on June 1. But my father doesn't need to know that. "Something to consider."

"You're so close to having it all, CJ."

"Thank you, sir."

"I mean that. You're an asset to the firm."

"Thank you, Father," I say, placing my glass on the starched white tablecloth and turning to face my dad. I drink up these words of praise gratefully.

He gives me a look. "Don't throw it all away on some—some—*artist*."

"For God's sake!"

"I'm just saying—"

"Why do you care?" I demand, the words unusually shrill and sharp for a conversation between me and my father.

"Now, CJ, I'm only—"

"I have no idea whom I'll end up with…whom I'll marry! But I mean to be open-minded, Father. I mean to be hopeful and optimistic, to start from the firm foundation of friendship and let love grow. I…I don't need a man to support me. We both know that I can support *him* if I need to—if I want to. I make well into six figures, and I'm not yet thirty. So, why does it matter? Why *the hell* do you care?"

"Smooth your feathers, CJ. Smooth them out now, miss."

"I'm sorry I yelled," I say, thinking of my future spouse. "Just…keep an open mind. Please."

He looks away from me with a heavy sigh, cocking his head to the side as he watches my mother and Josh dancing.

"Well, I suppose you could do worse. He's certainly charming. And very good-looking. At least your children would be—"

"Father!" I exclaim, feeling beyond exasperated. "How many times do I have to say it? I'm not *with* Josh."

He turns to me, his eyes narrowing. "Are you sure?"

I've heard that tone before. It's the voice he uses before cinching a major deal. It's the voice that lets his opponent know they've been bested. But I have no clue why he's using it now, with me.

My coiled muscles relax as I stare at him, trying to

figure out what the hell he's talking about. "What does *that* mean?"

"Nothing," he says, shaking his head.

He stares at me thoughtfully for a moment, before his attention is distracted by the woman sitting on his other side. She wants to know what he thought of the recent first-selectman elections, which gives me the perfect excuse to leave the table and step outside.

The patio door closes behind me, and I walk down a small set of stairs to the club's great lawn. Before me is a glorious view of Long Island Sound, dotted with expensive sail boats in the foreground and grand mansions standing proudly behind them across the water. I've been to this yacht club many times in my life—for regattas and parties, weddings and brunches—and the view has always calmed my spirit and soothed my soul.

But not tonight.

I grip the stem of my wineglass tighter.

Are you sure?

My father's words repeat in my head.

Are you sure? Are you sure? Are you sure?

"I'm *not* with Josh," I whisper to myself, strolling toward the water's edge. "Why is that so hard to understand?"

A lone bell chimes in the evening breeze, and I look up at the sky, at the thousands of stars on display.

Maybe it was my defense of Josh that led him to such a conclusion? The way I insisted that Josh was talented and hardworking? Or maybe it was the way I kept calling him my "friend" and then told my father that I want my future marriage to start from a foundation of friendship.

Hmm. Yes. In retrospect, I can see how my words could have misled my father. But I wasn't talking about Josh, of course. I was talking about my—

"Courtney."

I turn around to find Josh, tall and handsome in the moonlight, standing on the lawn behind me.

"Hi," I say, feeling my lips tilt up in an effortless smile because I'm so happy to see him.

"Your mom's a good dancer."

"Yes. She loves it."

"How about you?"

"No, thank you."

"You don't like dancing?"

I shrug, still a little bothered by the exchange with my father. I'm not ready to go back inside yet.

"You don't know how?" he asks, grinning at me.

"Of course I know how. My mother insisted on ballroom dance lessons."

"So, dance with me," he says, taking a step closer. He holds out his hand, and I consider saying no, but I can't think of a good reason why.

"Fine," I say, putting my hand in his and letting him pull me into his arms.

The song playing inside is "The Way You Look Tonight," crooned by a Benny Goodman-style troubadour, and it's always been one of my very favorites. I look into Josh's eyes as he settles one hand on my lower back and curls his fingers over the hand he's holding. I flatten my other palm on his shoulder and stand so close to him that I can smell his soap or aftershave. It's fresh and clean, and without meaning to, I find myself memorizing the scent, so that this night will come winging back to me should I ever smell it again.

My cheek brushes his jawline as we start moving, swaying gently to the beautiful words about a man, deeply in love with a woman, who pledges he'll never forget "the way she looks tonight."

"I love this song," I whisper.

"Courtney," says Josh, his voice low and my name gritty on his tongue.

"Hmm?"

He shifts his hand in mine so that our fingers are braided together. "What do you know about the matchmaking service you're using? Where'd you find them?"

"Oh. Um, on TV. And then online."

"You're sure they're reputable?"

I nod. "I believe so. They're affiliated with Lifetime TV. I looked up the experts on Wikipedia, and they seemed legit."

"What if—what if they don't actually match you well? What if they just send you the name of some guy?"

"Of course they're going to send me the name of some guy," I say, resting my chin on the hand that's on top of his shoulder and closing my eyes. "That's the whole point."

"But what if he's not right for you?"

"He will be."

Josh growls softly, then clears his throat. "You're really, um, committed to this."

"Mm-hm. I am. I am committed to it. One hundred percent." I lean away a little bit, so I can look into his eyes. "That's the only way it'll work."

His face is troubled—so troubled, in fact, it makes my heart skip a beat, because I can't account for it. "What? What's wrong?"

He clenches his jaw, moving his hand from my lower back to my waist to hold me a little tighter. "I just—I don't want you to get hurt."

"But that's exactly why I'm doing this," I explain to him. "Because I don't want to be hurt anymore either."

He stares at me for a beat before nodding. "Okay. Got it."

I'm eager to change the subject and remember I don't know where he's from. "Where did you grow up?"

"A little town outside of Minneapolis called Minnetonka."

"Minnesota. I wouldn't have guessed."

"Why not?"

"Don't Minnesotans have a midwestern accent?"

"Oh, ya. Fer sure they do."

I giggle. "You lost yours?"

"I've been here for almost a decade." He laughs softly. "I got a scholarship to NYU and never went home."

"Never?"

"I've gone home for visits. But I never moved back."

"Your family must miss you."

"I go home for Christmas. And we talk every Sunday afternoon."

"You and your parents?"

He nods. "Uh-huh. They call me when they get home from church."

"So, you're close to them?"

"I can't pop around for a cup of sugar, but yeah, we've stayed close."

"That sounds nice," I murmur, placing my cheek on his shoulder as the band plays the last verse of the song.

I'm pressed up against Josh, and it occurs to me how solid he is under his tux. I know he's athletic because I've seen his muscles—not to mention that time a couple of weeks ago when he vaulted across the bar. But it's unexpectedly wonderful to be held like this in his arms, with my chest flush against his. He smells wonderful, and he's a good friend to me. And suddenly, I hope that the experts choose someone like Josh for me—someone with all Josh's best traits, but who's looking for marriage, for forever, *for me* and everything I have to offer the right man.

"I have two tickets for *Miss Saigon*," he says. "From a— a, um, friend of mine. Next Saturday. Come with me?"

"Oh, I'd love to!" I say, leaning back to smile up at him.

"It's your favorite," he says softly, his eyes serious as he looks down into mine. I can hear his breathing, shallow and shaky, as puffs of warm breath fall softly on my cheek.

"You remembered."

The song has ended, and we're not dancing anymore; we're just standing in each other's arms under a thousand twinkling stars.

His eyes dart to my lips and linger there. "Yes."

Kiss me.

The thought streaks through my mind like lightning, unexpected and startling. But on its heels is another, stronger thought:

You're going to ruin everything, Courtney! Step away right now, miss!

He leans closer.

"Courtney—"

His lips are a breath away from mine.

"I think you should take me back inside," I say quickly. "I think that would be best."

He groans softly, almost a sound of pain. From this close, I can see his jaw clench as he releases my hand and steps away.

My eyes are suddenly burning, and I blink them, feeling unaccountably miserable to lose the warmth and safety of his arms.

He nods once, then gestures to the stairs with his hand and whispers, "After you."

***

When I wake up in my parents' house the next morning, the first thing I think about when my eyes open is Josh.

In my half-dream state, I picture how he looked in his tuxedo, standing by the clock at Grand Central Station. He stole my breath with his handsome smile, with the way he looked at me as I approached him.

I remember how it felt to hold hands with him on the

train, how wonderful it made me feel to know he thought I was beautiful and smart, kind and funny.

My mind slides to my father's subtle question, which deftly undermined all my declarations about our "friendship" status: *Are you sure?*

I cannot deny the fact that I wanted Josh to kiss me on the lawn. Even if I wanted it only for a split second. I wanted to feel his lips on mine. I wanted to taste him, to feel the satin slide of his tongue against mine, to know the feeling of his body pressed intimately, without reserve, with passion, against mine.

And I recall how it felt to say good-bye when a taxi collected him at the club; how sad I felt to see him go, and how I wished that I was leaving with him.

It all adds up to one thing, one thing I wish I could refute but can't.

"Stop fooling yourself and admit it," I whisper, rolling onto my back. "You feel more for him than friendship."

Stupid girl that I am, I'm less than a month away from meeting my future husband, and I've developed a full-blown crush on Josh-the-bartender, Josh-the-playwright, Josh…the wonderful.

"Shit. Fuck. Poop," I mutter, staring up at the pristine white ceiling of my childhood bedroom. "Fantastic work, Courtney. You're falling for Josh. You are *such* an idiot."

I pull one of my pillows over my face and scream into it, but swearing and screaming give me no peace. I need to take action. I need to do something to right this wrong, because it almost feels like I'm cheating on my fiancé, and

I'm *not* a cheater. I won't be made one by Josh Dalton.

Grabbing my phone off the nightstand, I pull up Josh's number—the one he called me back on from the New Dramatists last Monday—and I open a message screen. Swinging my legs over the side of the bed, I stare at the screen, trying to figure out what to say.

Hi, Josh. It's Courtney.

I tap enter.

Thank you for being my escort to the Frederick wedding. It was very kind of you, and everyone thought you were very charming. Don't be surprised if Simi contacts you about her drama festival in Boston this fall.

I tap enter again, taking a deep breath. Now for the heart of the matter.

I type *I can't see you anymore*, then erase it because it feels incredibly overdramatic.

I try again. *I know I'm a fool, but my feelings for you (despite our mutual agreement to be friends) are outgrowing friendship, and I can't seem to stop wanting—*

"No!" I hiss, deleting the letters. "He doesn't deserve to have you spew emotional vomit all over him either!"

Taking a deep breath, I flip over my phone and think for a second. Am I overreacting? I mean, we *didn't* actually kiss. We held hands on the train, and we danced at a wedding. Friends hold hands sometimes, don't they? And everyone dances at weddings. Am I making too big a deal out of this?

Besides, if actions speak louder than words, all I need to do is avoid him. I won't go to Tidewaters for the next three or four Fridays, until after I'm matched. If I can do that—

My phone dings with a message alert.

It was my pleasure. I'm looking forward to seeing Miss Saigon with you on Saturday.

Oh, shit!

I totally forgot that I agreed to go to a show with him.

"Shit, shit, shit!" I say, throwing the phone on my bed and crossing my bedroom to plop down on my window seat. It looks out over our family estate, and in the distance, I can see the horses in the paddock out for an early morning grazing.

My phone dings again, and I'm up like a shot, racing back to my bed.

Meet me at the theater at 7:45?

I stare at the words, wondering if I should cancel. But that seems like it would be really mean and ungrateful, now that I've said yes and he already has the tickets. Especially after he's done me the favor of being my escort last night.

Hmm. Maybe all I need to do is reconfirm our status as friends. Maybe that would be enough to curb my feelings and make it clear to him that nothing has changed, despite the hand-holding and moonlight-dancing and almost-kisses.

I'll see you at 7:45 next Saturday, I write, and then add, *I'm lucky to have a friend like you.*

I sit on the edge of my bed, waiting for an answer, my knee bobbing up and down with nerves. Will he reject the word "friend"? Will he refuse it? And why—oh, why?—is there a part of me that hopes he does?

Seconds turn into minutes that drag by at the speed of

molasses in January until finally—

Ding.

I flip over my phone, and peek with bated breath to find a thumbs-up emoji.

And if there was ever a girl more disappointed to see a goddamned thumbs-up emoji in her entire life, I'd like to meet her.

CHAPTER 8

<u>Josh</u>

I'm lucky to have a friend like you.

I flinch at the words, staring at them with vitriol as I pour the fourth of four coffees, slip my phone into my apron pocket, and take the mugs to a waiting brunch table.

"Here are your coffees," I say to the four-top of girls in their twentysomethings sitting on the patio in the sunshine. "Can I get anyone a mimosa or a bloody mary?"

One girl, curled up in her chair, lowers her sunglasses to get a better look at me. She licks her lips and grins. "You're cute."

"Thanks."

"What are you doing later?"

"Amelia! Oh, my God!" One of her friends lightly slaps her knee while the other two giggle. "You're such a slut!"

"I'm noooot," she insists, smiling wider at me. "So?"

I sigh. She's cute. And she's obviously DTF. But I'm not interested, which is so fucked up, I can barely get my head around it.

"Sorry. I'm busy," I say, winking at her to soften the blow.

She makes a face. "Busy, or taken?"

I am not taken. I am definitely not taken by anyone, least of all by a woman naïve enough to think that an arranged marriage is her best option for happiness!

"Busy," I hear myself mutter.

"Sure about that?" she asks, raising an eyebrow.

"No."

"Sounds complicated." She chuckles softly, grabs a ballpoint pen from my apron and reaches for my hand. After she writes "Amelia" and her phone number on my palm, she puts a heart around it. "I tell you what—I'm *not* complicated. If you're still not sure when you get off work, text me."

With a dry smile, I pull my hand away.

"Was that yes or no on the mimosas?"

They all order one, and I turn around, walking back inside Tidewaters to make their drinks.

Last night at the wedding, I had almost kissed Courtney after our dance on the lawn, and now I wish I fucking had. I had a shit night of sleep, dreaming about her and wishing I was making love to her all night long. I woke up hard, and even after I made myself come, my relief was only hollow.

I growl softly as I pour orange juice into four champagne flutes, then top it off with cava. Before I take the drinks outside, I wash my hand, using dish soap to scrub off most of the ink. It's ridiculous, but one, I'm not supposed to fuck the customers; two, if I took Amelia up on her offer, I think I might feel like I cheated on Courtney. Probably because I like her. I really*, really* like her.

I like her so much that I bought two tickets to *Miss*

Saigon last night with money I really don't have, even with my New Dramatists discount. Probably a waste of money, when the girl I'm taking will be married to someone else in a matter of weeks.

It's not a waste, my heart whispers as I head back outside with the drinks.

Sitting next to Courtney for almost three hours in a dark theater? Listening to my favorite Broadway love song, "Sun and Moon," with her beside me? Maybe even convincing her to take a walk around the moonlit streets of Manhattan with me when the show is over?

It's worth it.

I serve the drinks quickly, careful not to engage with the ladies at the table any further.

The website Courtney's using said that they generally match people within four to six weeks of receiving their application, which means that Courtney should be matched by June at the latest. Next month.

And come on, there's no way I'm going to have a hit play in a month. The sad reality, and one I wish I could change, is that we want different things in life: she wants the white-picket-fence dream deluxe as soon as possible, and I need to concentrate on workshopping my play into a successful Broadway show, which could take years. Our life goals are incompatible no matter how much she touches my heart.

So what option do I have?

To be her—fuck, I am growing to hate this word—*friend* until she meets her husband. And then? Fade to black, let her go, and just hope that I made the right choice. Just hope that choosing my career over Courtney isn't something I regret for the rest of my life.

***

On Saturday evening as I stand outside the Lunt-Fontanne theater, twenty minutes early to my meeting with Courtney, I think about last night. For the first time in months, she didn't show up at Tidewaters.

I'd kept watching the door and waiting for her to walk in, my heart bunching every time I thought I caught a glimpse of her and disappointment relaxing my muscles when I'd realized it wasn't her.

Dina had finally sauntered in around seven and made her way to the bar, and I experienced a small hit of elation— not to see Courtney's friend, but because I hoped Courtney wouldn't be far behind.

"Hey!" Dina shouted over the cacophony. "How about an Amstel?"

"Sure thing!" I answered. "And a gimlet?"

"A what? Oh! No, no need. Courts isn't coming."

Just like that, my stomach dropped. The girl I wanted to see—who I'd been *waiting* to see since last Saturday night— wasn't coming. And the thought that followed it? Sheer panic. What if she'd been matched? What if—right this minute—she was e-mailing her future husband, making plans for their anonymous *fucking* wedding?

I clenched my jaw and stared down at the chrome bar, feeling miserable. "Why?"

"Why what?"

"Where is she? Why isn't she coming?"

"She's not feeling…"

I looked up to find Dina's mouth open and eyes wide. It only took a second to realize she'd been catching the play-by-play of my feelings as they sailed across my face.

"Holy shit! Josh!"

"No," I muttered, shaking my head.

"Yes!"

"No, Dina." I reached down for an Amstel light, popped off the cap, and placed it on the bar with a frosted pint glass.

"Yes, yes, yes, Josh! Oh, my God! How did I not see this before now?"

I rested my hands on my hips. "See what? What do you *think* you're seeing?"

"*Think?* No, darling—I *know* what I'm seeing. You *like* her," said Dina gravely, sliding onto a barstool freed up by a guy whose friends had arrived. She leaned forward. "You're *sad* she's not here. You're *into* her."

I stared at her for a second, trying to figure out what to say. Finally, I shrugged, shaking my head with frustration and confusion. "I don't know what I am."

"Oh, my God, Josh. This is so super cute. You *like* her."

I do. She's right. There's no sense in denying it.

"Doesn't matter," I said, taking an empty pint glass from a guy behind Dina and refilling it with an IPA on tap.

"Did you know that she's…" Dina's voice tapered off as her dark brown eyes looked into mine. Hers were soft.

Sympathetic. Kind. "She might not be available much longer."

"Yeah," I said, taking a twenty from the guy and giving him back ten. "I know."

"You do? She told you? About her arranged-marriage plan?"

I rolled my eyes and sighed. "Yeah."

"And apparently you feel the same way about it that I do."

"How can someone so smart do something so stupid?"

Dina took a big sip of beer, tossing a look over her shoulder. "She's sick of this."

"Who isn't? That's no reason to marry a complete stranger."

"Not in New York, anyway," agreed Dina, flipping her jet-black hair from one shoulder to another. "Too many crazies. But I can't talk her out of it. If anything, every time we talk, she feels empowered, because my parents were successfully matched."

"Then *please* stop talking to her," I begged Dina.

"You *like* her."

Ever since the moment she uttered the word "marriage," I've felt this almost otherworldly pull toward Courtney. And if I had the guts to examine why, I might realize that Courtney's articulating something I want for myself, too. Marriage—the certainty, the inherent partnership, the unconditional love, the promise of a sweet forever—is something that I want also.

Someday, I quickly amend as I think back on it. *Not now, but someday.*

I had been unwilling to share those deep thoughts with Dina last night, so instead I'd said: "I feel protective of her. She's a good person. I don't want to see her get hurt."

"Because you like her."

"Yes. Fine. I like her."

"What are you doing about it?"

"What do you mean?"

"To stop her. What are you doing? Why don't you ask her out?"

"We've been out," I replied. "We're *friends.*"

"Josh, I'm not an idiot. Your face doesn't read 'friends.' It reads 'get-in-my-bed-and-stay-there, you-hot-slice-of-woman'!"

In spite of how crappy I'd felt, I laughed. "You know her. She's antidating. She would rather marry a stranger than date another person. And I'm…" I blew out an exasperated breath. "I'm into her, yes. But come on. I'm not ready to get married. To anyone."

And Dina? Dina, who'd fought Courtney tooth and nail about arranged marriage only two weeks before, looked up at me from under thick, black lashes and asked:

"Why not?"

And it's *that* question that's buzzing around in my brain as, here and now, I stand outside of *Miss Saigon*, waiting for Courtney.

Why not?

Every good reason in the world rushes to my mind.

First and foremost?

Because I'm not ready.

I'm not ready to be a provider like my dad. By the time he was my age, he was a junior accountant with a solid health care plan and potential for growth. He had a wife and toddler at home and another on the way. By contrast, I live in an apartment with four other people, and some months, when I need to pay for a performance venue or ad space in a drama festival program, my finances are so tight that I have less than twenty dollars in my bank account after paying rent.

I'm not ready to be tied down. I like flirting with random girls at Tidewaters. Chalking up as an anomaly the fact that I haven't even been able to look at another woman since I started having feelings for Courtney, I've always liked keeping my options open. Am I really ready to be with one woman for the rest of my life?

And last but not least, Courtney and I as a unit aren't ready. Sure, we've *technically* known each other for over a year, but we've only gotten closer recently. Most people I know date for years and then live together, to be sure they have a solid basis for forever. Frankly, at this point, Courtney and I would have little better than an arranged marriage ourselves, were we to get together.

I'm just not husband material in any real or traditional sense, and trying to act like I am is just going to end up hurting both of us by killing my dreams and disappointing a woman who deserves the best of everything life has to offer. And I refuse to do either.

I lean against the cement wall of the Lunt-Fontanne theater, watching cabs drop off passengers who are either on their way to a show or out for a night on the town. A misty rain is falling, and it lands in tiny droplets on my lashes and cheeks. A bus honks its horn as a scalper tries to sell me tickets, and I think to myself, *I love it here. This is a good life, isn't it?*

I turn to the left to inhale the smell of hot dogs and roasted chestnuts and then—

And then I see her.

I see Courtney Jane Salinger walking toward me.

She's holding an umbrella, and her blonde hair, like liquid honey, tumbles around her shoulders in waves. Her dress is royal-blue silk and short, but what really draws my attention are the knee-high, brown-suede boots she's wearing. They allow a strip of skin to peek out between the tops of the boots and the bottom of the dress. And—*fuck me*—but how I *covet* that skin. I want to kill every man who's checking out that strip of skin, because I want it to belong to *me*.

I force my gaze up, over the hem of her unbuttoned khaki trench coat, lingering on her full breasts before finally landing on her smile. She's like a tractor beam—and I know the definition of "tractor beam" because I just looked it up to see if it's an appropriate phrase to use in my play. First coined for science fiction novels, it's a beam of light that attracts one object to another over a distance. She's the beam of light. She's *my* beam of light, and I'm attracted. I can't fucking look away.

One hand holds an umbrella, and she raises the other in greeting as she comes closer. I feel mine lift from my side, like she's bidden it gently to respond in kind, and it must comply.

"Hi," she says, stopping before me. Her voice is breathy like she's been running, except I know she hasn't been.

I want to say something. I *mean* to speak, but I can't. I can't say anything. I just stand there staring at her—so glad to see her, so furious at her for this arranged-marriage bullshit, so angry that I like her as much as I do, and so fucking sad that our time together isn't limitless.

She scans my eyes with hers for a second and then steps closer, reaching for me, and drawing me into her lilac-scented arms for a hug hello. Touch. It's an aphrodisiac. It's a promise of something without giving everything. My body reacts where my mouth cannot, and I pull her against me, shaking inside, my eyes closing in surrender as she leans her cheek against my shoulder.

And that's how we stand, holding each other in front of the Lunt-Fontanne theater; opponents with a small respite from a terrible war, with only one another for support. I can't have her. She can't have me. Damn you, fate and attraction and everything else that has hurled us into outer space together, two celestial bodies gravitationally pulled to one another, for better or worse.

Still holding her tight, I lean down a little so that my lips are close to her ear.

"Hey," I whisper. "How're you feeling? Dina said you were under the weather."

"Better," she says, still resting against me. I can't lie—

the hint of congestion in her voice makes me weirdly happy. I was worried she was avoiding me last night. And if she's really got a cold, it proves she wasn't.

"I missed you last night," I admit. "At least two gimlets went to waste when I thought I saw you in the crowd."

"Poor gimlets," she says, leaning away. She cocks her head to the side and smiles up at me. "Someday I'm going to get a cat and name him Gimlet."

"To remind you of your wasted days in New York?" I ask, but my real question is: *To remind you of me?*

"Not wasted," she whispers, her voice earnest and soft. "Never wasted."

Her smile turns sad, and she straightens. My arms loosen as she steps out of my embrace.

"This will be my third time seeing this show," I tell her, gesturing for her to precede me into the theater.

"Mine too!" she exclaims, grinning at me over her shoulder.

Oh, my heart. My stupid, reckless heart.

I feel it. In that moment, I *know* it.

I'm falling for her. No matter how much I don't want to, no matter how much our timing sucks, no matter how little time we have—I'm falling hard and fast, and I have a feeling there's nothing I can do about it now.

I show our tickets to the usher, who waves us inside.

"Did I hear him right?" asks Courtney. "Did he say 'Orchestra, Row B'?"

I nod. What can I say? I splurged. I wanted her to have the best seats in the whole damn house. I just wanted to do this one stupid thing for her.

"Josh!" Her smile is blinding. "I've never sat so close. Thank you."

I can't help myself. I take her hand in mine, grateful beyond measure when she doesn't pull it away.

Moments later, seated side by side in the dark, our fingers are still linked together, though we haven't looked at each other since I took her hand, as though meeting each other's eyes would break the spell we're under.

Soon we are swept away on a tale of forbidden love between an American soldier and Vietnamese bar girl during the American occupation of Vietnam in in the 1970s. The eighth musical number is called "Sun and Moon"; a love song between the hero and heroine in which they speak of their differences—or rather, of how, in spite of those differences, they have fallen in love with one another. She calls him "sunlight" and herself "moon," and the two are joined by "the gods of fortune."

Unable to stop myself, I turn and look at Courtney, who lifts her chin before twisting her neck just a touch to meet my eyes. Lifting her hand to my lips, I press them to her skin while my eyes, no doubt black and shiny as they seize hers in the darkness, try to tell her everything my voice can't.

You're my sun, I think. *My dreams are the earth, and I'm the moon.*

I recall a little-known fact: the earth's moon is the only permanent, natural object in the solar system on which the sun has a stronger gravitational influence than the planet the moon orbits.

Briefly, fleetingly, I wonder if it's possible that my attraction to Courtney—my fierce gravitational pull to be near her, to both possess and belong to her—could prove stronger than my dreams.

And for the first time since I moved to New York—for a split second that will surely haunt me for the rest of my life—I don't know.

I don't know, and that terrifying sliver of doubt makes me lift my lips and release her hand. Her eyebrows furrow together in confusion, but I look away, focusing my attention on Chris and Kim, whose passionate, reckless love affair in Vietnam will lead to tragedy.

***

"So, how was viewing number three?" I ask as the applause die down, and the house lights come up.

Her eyes are red, and tears make her cheeks glisten. "I always hope that the ending will be different. I get it that Chris went home from Vietnam and married Ellen, but he loves Kim, too. When he and Ellen go back to Vietnam, I wish—I just wish he'd have chosen Kim."

"Over his wife?"

She sighs. "Kim's the mother of his son. He made her a lot of promises. There's an argument to be made that Chris *should* choose her over Ellen."

"Do you think Chris knew Ellen before he left for Vietnam?" I ask her.

"Does it matter?"

I stand up, leaning down to pick up her umbrella and

offering it to her as she stands up.

"Yes," I say. "Maybe Ellen was his first love. Maybe dreams of her—the girl back at home—were what got him through Vietnam."

"Dreams can change," she says, taking the umbrella from me as we step sideways out from our row into the congested aisle.

She walks in front of me, and I trace the delicate line of her neck with my eyes, hungry to memorize it, though it will only torture me later, as memories of Kim tortured Chris once he returned to America.

Back outside, the rain is coming down heavier, and Courtney opens her umbrella.

"Get under!" she says.

I duck underneath, standing close to her. "Let's go for a drink and see if it lets up?"

She nods, and I put my arm around her shoulders, leading her away from the theater and around the block to the Rum House, one of my favorite spots in the ultratouristy Broadway district. It may look sketchy on the outside, but with its dark wood, red leather banquet tables, and creative cocktail list, it's a piece of old-time Broadway heaven in the middle of Disney-fied Times Square, and I love it.

I hold open the door and she rushes in, turning around to smile at me with eyes brightened by our dash through the rain. "Where are we?"

"The Rum House."

"A real, live dive," she says, looking around with approval.

My friend Godwin is at the piano with his partner, Rosy, who's finishing up a slow and sultry rendition of "Can't Help Lovin' Dat Man" from *Showboat*.

I gesture to an empty table in the corner. "Grab it for us? I'll go get us drinks. A gimlet, I assume?"

But she surprises me by shaking her head. "New bar, new drink. Pick something for me!"

I watch her sidle through a small group of people, then I turn to the bar, waving at my friend Hannah, who was with me at NYU.

"Josh! Where are you coming from?" She leans over the bar and kisses my cheek.

"*Miss Saigon.*"

"Ooooo! Good times. Won't be around much longer, either."

"Yeah, I heard. Revival's almost ready to go on tour."

Hannah looks over my shoulder. "Who's that?"

"Friend."

"Hmm." She grins. "What are you and your friend having tonight?"

"She told me to surprise her."

Hannah nods sagely. "And you saw *Miss Saigon* tonight?"

"That's right."

"Are we trying to impress your 'friend'?"

I shrug.

"I got you covered," she says. "Go sit. I'll have Manny bring them over."

"You're the best," I say, putting a twenty in the tip jar

because I know she won't let me pay her for the first round.

As I pass by Rosy, she grins at me and waves, finishing up her song to a round of polite applause.

"Joshy!" she says. "I saw you come in!"

"We ducked in to get out of the rain."

"Have a request?" she asks, glancing in Courtney's direction. "You name it. I'll sing it."

"*Love Never Dies?*" I ask.

"Coming right up," she says, winking at me.

I make my way to Courtney, sliding into the round booth beside her. "Hi."

"Are you a regular?"

"I don't know about a regular, but Hannah and I went to school together."

"And the singer?"

"Rosy? She and Godwin have been a fixture here for years. Hannah introduced me to them."

"They're fond of you."

"What's not to love?" I ask, winking at her.

She laughs at me. "Where'd you learn to be so charming?"

"Better tips," I tell her, reaching for the bowl of nuts on the table and taking a handful. "You get better tips if you flirt."

"Aha! It's all about financial gain, huh? I can respect that."

Manny stops by our table with two bright-red drinks in martini-style glasses, each garnished with an orange slice, maraschino cherry, and little paper umbrella. "Thanks,

Manny."

"What is *this*?" asks Courtney, her eyes sparkling as Godwin starts playing the opening notes of Andrew Lloyd Webber's masterpiece "Love Never Dies," from his *Phantom of the Opera* sequel of the same name.

"I have no idea," I admit, leaning down and taking a sip. "But whatever it is, it's—"

"Delicious," we say at the same time.

"Who knows when love begins?" sings Rosy, *"Who knows what makes it start?"*

We both turn toward the music, and without being creepy, I watch Courtney as Rosy sings, wondering if this song that I love so terribly will touch her heart as well. It doesn't take long for her lips to part and her eyes to widen as the song swells with words about a forever love that will never die, that will even outlast those who experience it. When the song is over, Courtney dabs at her eyes, clapping loudly for Rosy, who nods at us and mouths, "You're welcome" before taking a break for water.

"Is this your life?" asks Courtney. "Broadway shows and divey bars and beautiful music?"

"And barely making rent, and never knowing if my dreams are in vain, and wondering if the day will come when I'll have to admit that it's never going to happen."

"Don't say that." She reaches for my hand. "It will happen, Josh. I believe in you."

"Why?"

"Because you're beautiful and smart, funny and kind," she says, echoing my compliments to her from last weekend.

"You're going to be a big hit someday, and I'll tell everyone I 'knew-you-when.'"

"Where will you be?" I ask her, a hollow feeling making my chest ache. "When all my dreams are coming true?"

Her smile falters for a minute, before she forces it into place. But she pulls her hand from mine. "Hopefully, I'll be happily married. Maybe with a baby on the way."

"White picket fence and a minivan?"

"Negotiable," she says.

"Really?" I ask, because this surprises me.

"I grew up in New York City until I was twelve," she says. "My parents always had a house in Greenwich for weekends and holidays, but our primary residence was here. They swapped that arrangement so I could go to middle school and high school in the suburbs."

"I didn't know."

"How would you?" she asks, taking another sip of Hannah's magical (and quite potent) rum punch. "Mmm! This is so yum—"

"Don't do it," I blurt out.

Her eyes meet mine. "Don't do what?"

Give me a chance! Give us time!

"Don't use the matchmaker service," I say.

She's staring back at me, and I realize that her expression is filling with hurt. "Why not? Why wouldn't you want me to be happy?"

"I *do* want you to be happy," I say.

"Then don't take my dream away from me, Josh. I'd never take yours away from you. Friends don't shatter each other's dreams. They look out for each other."

"Friends?" I scoff, feeling desperate, feeling angry.

"Yes," she says, confusion joining the hurt in her eyes. "Friends. We're friends, aren't we?"

"News flash, Courtney," I spit out. "Friends don't hold hands. They don't dance in the moonlight. They don't go on dates. They don't blow money they don't have on theater tickets. And when they're together, they don't have to fight against kissing each other with every bit of strength they have!"

She's staring at her drink, looking utterly distraught. Finally, she lifts her head, and the pain in her glistening eyes just about flattens me. "This was a mistake."

"No!" I say, reaching for her wrist as she pushes off from the seat and slides out of the booth, out of my grasp.

"I shouldn't have come tonight. I just—I'm so…"

"You just what?" I demand. "You're so what? Be honest with me, Courtney. Please!"

She plucks her purse from the tabletop. "I'm so sorry."

I could have jumped up and run after her. I could have grabbed her arm on the rainy sidewalk outside of the Rum House and turned her around. I could have dropped my lips to hers and kissed her with every ounce of feeling I have for her. And I could have hoped that she'd withdraw her application to be arranged and choose me instead.

Except that friends don't shatter each other's dreams, and if I can't make hers come true, I have no right to take them away.

CHAPTER 9

<u>Courtney</u>

I cry on the cab ride home to my apartment, then kick off my shoes, lie down on my bed, and cry some more.

Partially because I know that Josh is right: friends don't hold hands or have romantic dances in the moonlight or *fight against kissing each other with every bit of strength they have*. And partially because *not* articulating our magnetic attraction and burgeoning feelings meant that I could both enjoy it and deny it, and now I can't. I was happily eating my cake, and he took it away from me.

Now I have to confront my feelings and deal with them, something I really didn't want to do. Either that, or I need to make the blanket decision to stop spending time around Josh. With a fiancé in the process of being arranged for me, I shouldn't be spending time with a man for whom I've developed feelings. It's not fair to him, or to me, or to the man I'll be marrying soon.

"Gah! I hate my life!"

Leaving my bed, I blow my nose as I head to the kitchen to make myself a cup of tea. While I'm standing at the sink filling an old-fashioned kettle with water, my eyes land on the bullet-point list entitled "Prepare for Your Arranged Marriage," and I lean against the counter, feeling guilty.

Don't do it. Don't use the matchmaker service.

I blink my eyes against more tears when I hear his voice in my head.

Oh, my heart. My stupid, stupid heart.

It's such early days. Too early to feel this much. It's dangerous to let myself fall when there are no guarantees. No intentions have been declared. No commitment is in place. We're still a ways away from calling each other boyfriend and girlfriend. And then what? There's the meeting-each-other's-friends stage. And the moving-in-together stage. And the meeting-each-other's-family stage. The splitting-holidays stage. The fights. The breakups. The "I love yous." The makeups. And then—maybe, just maybe—if he doesn't get bored of me and move to LA with the twentysomething cutie pie starring in his play, we might end up engaged and then married. But how many years from now? Two? Three? Ten?

The kettle whistles, and I jump.

"You can't do this to yourself," I mutter, opening the cabinet next to the stove and taking out a teabag, which I throw into a mug and chase with boiling water. "You *have* a plan. A good plan. A plan that sidesteps years of terrible worrying and wondering and heartbreak."

So that's that.

Ignore your feelings. Avoid Josh. Be arranged. Get married.

I take my tea into the living room and plop down on

the couch, covering myself with a fleecy blanket.

But what if it doesn't take two years or three or ten? asks a voice in the back of my mind. *What if you ignore what you feel and walk away from Josh when he could've made you happy?*

I was serious tonight when I said he was beautiful and smart, funny and kind. And he *is* my friend, but he's also become so much more than that. The way he held me in his arms when I arrived at the theater tonight. The way he kissed my hand during "Sun and Moon." My breath hitches, and I exhale on a sob. I have feelings for him. *Real* feelings. When I think of him spending money he doesn't have on those tickets just to spend time with me, it makes me want to weep for days.

I reach for my tea, sniffling pathetically as I take a sip. Then I lean back on the couch, remembering his voice near my ear when he told me that he missed me last night. *At least two gimlets went to waste when I thought I saw you in the crowd...*

I wake up hours later on the couch, my eyes still burning from tears, and my heart so heavy with doubt and confusion, I wonder how my chest can contain it.

***

Burying myself in work, I burn the candle at both ends this week, arriving at the office early and leaving after nine every night. Josh doesn't call or text, which feels good and bad for different reasons, but makes it easier for me to tunnel into work. Hell, I'm woman enough to admit that now and then, when I'm truly overwhelmed, avoidance is one of my chosen tactics for dealing with uncomfortable personal issues.

By Friday, however, I'm not only avoiding my feelings

for Josh, I'm also avoiding Dina. If I run into her at the office, I know she'll try to get me to go out tonight. But if I can skip Tidewaters this week and next, I'll make it to the June 1 deadline without seeing Josh again. It makes me sad to think of leaving things between us on such a sour note, but I know it's the smarter choice. He can't give me what I want, and if I were to compromise—to give him a chance and date him—only to find myself alone and unmarried five years from now? I'd never forgive myself…or him.

My "Avoid + Ignore" plan is going really well, in fact, until four thirty, when my assistant, Pam, buzzes me over the intercom.

"Miss Khatri is calling. Mr. DeWitt would like to see you before you leave for the day."

"Thanks, Pam. Tell Dina I'll stop by Walter's office in half an hour."

Shoot. There goes my plan to avoid Dina until sneaking out of here at five. Oh, well.

I admit I'm curious as to why Walter DeWitt, the founder and CEO of DeWitt, Morris & Jones, wants to see me. My day-to-day dealings are mostly with Joel Morris, our CFO. I head to the ladies' room to freshen up, then return to my office to pack up for the day. With any luck, I'll miss Dina and beeline straight to the elevator after my meeting. I bid Pam a good weekend, then begin my trek across the building to Walter's office, which sits in the southwest corner of the building and affords knockout views of the sunset over the Hudson River. All the trappings of success and power.

When I arrive at Walter's suite of offices, Dina is sitting at her desk. She looks up and offers me a warm smile.

"Hey, stranger!"

"Hey, Dina," I say, grinning at her. Her glossy black hair is pulled back in a ponytail, and she's wearing a sapphire-blue silk blouse. "Great color for you."

"Jewel tones," she says. "An Indian girl's best friend."

I gesture to Walter's office. "Do you know what this is about?"

"Nope. But you can tell me all about it over drinks. I'll run to the ladies while you're inside and we can head downstairs as soon as you're finished."

"Oh. No, I don't think so. Not tonight, Dee."

"What?" She pouts. "Why not? We always—"

"I'm tired. I've got stuff to—"

"One drink. Come on! I don't want to go alone."

"You're never *alone*," I say. "You'll have ten guys swarming you five minutes after you arrive."

Dina bites her bottom lip, then tilts her head to the side, her dark eyes holding on to my blue. "I talked to Josh last week."

Just his name. Just hearing his name sends a shiver of pleasure mixed with melancholy down my spine.

"Oh." I gulp, searching her face, thirsty for any and all news about Josh.

"He really likes you."

My heart clutches.

"I like him too," I admit in a whisper.

"Then, Court—"

"*Like* isn't enough," I say. "Don't you get it? I'm on the precipice of *forever.*"

"Or disaster."

"Thanks a lot."

"I don't share your optimism about this matchmaking business," Dina shoots back. "I've been up front about that with you."

"I'd like your support."

"Can't give it," says Dina. "Josh is real. Josh is a known entity. I'd choose that over the unknown any day. Besides, he's sweet and he's hot and he likes you. Isn't that enough to give him a chance?"

"No," I say, crossing my arms over my chest. "I've really thought about this, and no, it isn't. The reason I signed up with ArrangeMeToo.com in the first place is that I'm done dating. My heart can't take it. And that's just dating *random* guys. If I date Josh, who I actually *care* about, and it goes sour? I'll not only have wasted years of my life, it'll be…devastating." I pause, remembering the plot to *Great Expectations*, which I read in high school. A woman disappointed by a jilted marriage locks herself up in a mansion and essentially becomes a hermit for the rest of her life because she can't and won't trust her heart to be broken again. "I could become another Miss Havisham."

"A what?"

"Never mind."

Dina tsks, then purses her lips and shakes her head at me. "Court, I'm worried about you."

"Don't be. I have a plan."

"I know all about your stupid plan. That's what worries me."

I shrug because we're at an impasse. She doesn't think ArrangeMeToo.com will work and I do. And I'm not letting her—or Josh—ruin it for me.

"How do you know you won't regret it?"

"My arranged marriage?"

"Fuck your arranged marriage!" she hisses, shooting a quick glance at Walter's closed door before continuing with her tirade. "No! Walking away from Josh. What if you regret it?"

"The only thing I'd regret is giving up my expert-arranged match to date someone for God only knows how long and end up alone and brokenhearted several years from now. Christ, Dee! Give it a break, okay? I'm doing this. It's *my* life!"

"Fine," says Dina. "Then come have a drink with me. If you're so sure you're making the right choice, then running into Josh shouldn't bother you, right? It shouldn't matter if you see him."

I take a deep breath and let it go slowly.

She has a point. It would be empowering to say hello to Josh, have a quick drink at the bar, and then go home. I could even apologize for running out on him last weekend and make peace with Josh so that he didn't take up so much of my mind. I could put our short little flirtation behind me and continue forward on my path with a clear conscience.

"Okay. I'll go."

Her intercom beeps. "Has Miss Salinger arrived yet?"

"I'll send her right in, sir," answers Dina.

Before I open Walter's door, I turn around.

One drink, I mouth to Dina, who nods, looking pleased as punch that she got her way.

One drink I hope I don't regret.

***

Four weeks in London.

That's what Walter wanted to talk to me about.

Whether or not I'd be open to spending the next month in London to look at prospects and make recommendations on initial investments.

"It's not a mandatory assignment, Miss Salinger," he said, "but it would bolster our confidence in you to know that you could step in on an international level now and then."

As Dina checks her phone beside me on the elevator ride to the lobby, I consider Walter's offer. I would have an apartment of my choosing and an ample allowance, and I would be paid an additional bonus for the four weeks. I'd leave as early as next Monday and return sometime in mid-June…just in time to get married.

Josh's face flitted through my mind when Walter suggested the trip, and I can't deny that I felt something tighten inside of me at the notion that tonight will likely be my final chance, as a single woman, to see him. It made my decision to get married by expert more real than ever.

But it also made me rise to Dina's challenge. *If you're so sure you're making the right choice, then running into Josh shouldn't bother you, right?* Right.

And yet, as we exit the elevator and breeze through the glass doors onto the sidewalk, a knot forms in my stomach.

As if she can sense my fear, Dina takes my arm, looping her elbow through mine. "It's okay to admit you've made a mistake."

I haven't.

"It's okay if you want to put your matchmaking service on hold. They'll still be there, ready to take your money."

"Actually, they have a clause about that," I tell her. "If you back out, you forfeit your money *and* there are no second chances, because it's an indication that you're not committed to the process."

"There are other matchmaking services in the world." She pauses. "My mother, for instance."

I laugh. "Does she have someone lined up for you?"

"Always," says Dina.

"What? I didn't know!"

She shrugs. "At least once a month I attend a very awkward dinner at my mummy's house wherein she's invited a *very eligible Indian bachelor* from *a very good family* to join us." She sighs. "I eat. He eats. We trade vitals. I feel bored. He eventually leaves. I tell my mummy no. She nods her head and sets up another dinner a few weeks later."

"Why don't you tell her to stop?"

"What do I have to lose? Maybe—just maybe—one night, my very own Punjabi prince charming will be sitting there across from me. And wouldn't I hate to miss out on that?"

She opens the door to Tidewaters, which is unusually

packed this evening, and I can't help it. My eyes zoom to the bar, where I catch a glimpse of Josh's dark head leaning over the long counter, talking to someone. Goosebumps break out across my arms.

There you are, my heart whispers.

I'm dumb struck for a moment, staring in his direction, feeling the corners of my lips turn up as he smiles at a customer, my eyes focused on the small dent of a dimple that appears in his cheek.

"Come on," says Dina, yanking on my arm.

"Where to? It's packed!"

"I think I see two seats at the end."

She elbows through the crowd, arriving at the end of the bar, where two guys are sitting side by side. Sidling up behind them, Dina lowers her voice and bats her lashes.

"Saving me and my friend a seat? You two are the sweetest."

The guys, whom I'm positive she doesn't know, turn in unison to look at her, and both smile instantly.

"Uh…yeah. That's, uh, exactly what we were doing," says Guy #1, sliding off his seat to offer it to her.

Dina giggles at him before turning to me. "Told you."

"Can we get you two some drinks?" asks Guy #2, offering me his stool.

"N—" I start to say, but Dina cuts me off.

"Sure. Thanks."

Feeling uneasy to be here, let alone to be accepting drinks from random guys, I slide onto the stool, staring down the bar at Josh. He's wearing a navy-blue T-shirt that hugs his chest and fits snugly over his biceps. Leaning over the bar to take an order, he cups his ear to hear better, then grins and nods. I watch as he picks up a pint glass and pulls down the lever on one of the draught beers, turning his head slowly to check out who else might be looking for service. When he gets to me, I'm waiting.

His eyes flare wide, and the casual smile on his face disappears. His lips tighten, and he stares at me until the beer he's pouring overflows onto his hand and he snaps his head back to see what he's doing. He mouths the word *Fuck*, then releases the valve and grabs a dishcloth to wipe the sides of the glass. As he puts the beer on a waiting cocktail napkin and slides it to the waiting patron, he glances my way again, his eyes dark and angry.

That's when I know.

I hurt him.

I hurt him when I left him at the Rum House, and that knowledge squeezes my heart in such a terrible way, I blink away tears as I stare down at the chrome counter.

A moment later, I hear his voice. "Hey, Hot Stuff. Amstel?"

"Yes, sir!" says Dina cheerfully, then more softly, "I brought Courts."

I look up at Josh, who offers me a cool smile that doesn't reach his eyes.

"What can I get for you?" he asks.

"A gimlet," I whisper.

He leans closer to me. "You sure? I wouldn't want you to make a *mistake*."

My words from last Saturday assault me: *This was a mistake.*

I swallow over the lump in my throat. "A gimlet, please."

"Their drinks are on me," says the guy standing next to Dina.

Josh turns his neck slowly to look at the guy, his eyes narrowing as he straightens up. "Who the fuck are you?"

"None of your business," says the guy. "Get the drinks, pal."

"I'm not your fucking pal," Josh growls, crossing his arms over his chest so the muscles on his arms pop.

The guy looks at his friend and laughs. "Fucking attitude on this guy, huh?"

"No tip for you!" his friend says to Josh in a singsong voice before winking at me.

Josh looks back and forth between them before looking back at me, his eyes confused. "Wait. Are you *with* these guys?"

"N-No! We just—"

The guy next to me sighs loudly. "What if she is, man? Seriously, can you just do your fucking job? An Amstel, a gimlet, two IPAs, and four tequila shots. Now."

Josh stares at me hard before sliding his eyes to the guy.

"Be careful," he says, flicking a mean glance at me before continuing. "This one will lead you on and then decide it's all a *mistake*." His nostrils flare like a bull about to impale a toreador. "I'll get you that drink, miss."

I can't bear his pain *or* his meanness; both hurt too

much. I close my eyes against the burn of tears about to fall and scramble for my bags. The only thing I can think about is getting out of there as soon as possible. I don't want to embarrass myself by crying in front of Josh.

"Hold up!" Dina grabs my arm. "Courts. Courtney! What are you doing?"

"I'm leaving."

"No. Come on. You promised to stay for one drink!"

I throw my purse and laptop bag over my shoulder and look up at her, unable to see her face clearly through my tears.

"Shit." Dina cringes at me. "I'll go with you."

"No. Don't make a scene. You stay."

"I'm not letting you—"

"*Please*," I beg her, blinking madly as I sidestep back from the bar and turn toward the door.

"Where's she going?" asks one of the guys as I push forward through the crowd.

"She's just upset. Don't—"

"Courtney!"

Josh's voice makes me turn around. I look over my shoulder to see him standing at the bar, his hands flat on the chrome counter, his eyes focused on me with a kind of wild severity. Suddenly, without warning, he does that vault-over-the-bar move, plowing through the crowd to catch up with me.

I get to the door, grateful when someone walking in holds it open for me, and I rush out onto the sidewalk just as hot rivulets start to streak down my cheeks.

"Courtney! Courtney, stop!"

I hear him behind me, calling my name, but I don't look back. I keep walking as fast as I can. Home isn't far, and once I'm home, I'm safe. I can cry my eyes out all night long.

But suddenly, I feel his hand on my arm. In an instant, he yanks me around, and I'm facing him, looking up into his fierce, furious eyes...

"Talk to me!"

...into his big, blue, beautiful eyes.

I don't think.

I act.

Standing on tiptoes, I reach around his neck and pull his face down to mine, arching my back as my lips touch his. He's startled at first, and his lips are slack and soft, though his body is rigid except for his chest—he's taking deep breaths after running to catch up with me. Each inhalation pushes his torso into mine, and I can feel his strength, how big and solid he is, rhythmically pressing into the softness of my breasts.

I flick my tongue over his closed lips, and a feral growl escapes from the back of his throat as his arms tighten suddenly around me. Now I am at his mercy as he holds me tightly, his lips moving hungrily over mine, his tongue sweeping into my mouth to taste me. I welcome the invasion, locking my fingers together behind his neck, my nipples pebbling into little stones inside my bra. I can feel the throbbing length of him bulging against my belly and try to get closer to him. I moan softly, and he swallows the sound before sliding his lips to the column of my throat. Hot kisses trail from my jawline to my collarbone as he whispers my name like a prayer.

"*Courtney, Courtney, Courtney*…I *knew* it could be like this," he murmurs, his voice deep and heavy, his breath warm against my skin.

"Yes," I breathe, tilting my head to the side so that he has better access to me, wanting his lips on every inch of my skin, on every tiny part of me.

He rests them on my pulse. "I can feel your heart. It's pounding."

I swallow, opening my eyes and wetting my lips for more.

He doesn't disappoint me.

His mouth crashes flush onto mine, and my lips are sealed with his as his tongue slides forward, velvet and warm, seeking its mate. He slides his hands to my backside, which he grabs and shoves forward roughly, against him, into his erection. The synapses in my brain fire, and a huge dopamine release makes me mold to him like jelly. The whole world is diluted to *this moment*, and at its center, at its core, beating its throbbing heart like a gong…are me and Josh.

His lips abandon mine, and I protest their loss with a whimper, my fingers tightening at the base of his neck.

"Jesus, Court," he sighs, leaning forward to nuzzle my nose with his. "Um. Let me…let me go back and punch out. Annie can, um, cover…"

He's still speaking, but his voice, talking about

punching out and shift coverage, vaults me from a place of dewy arousal to brutal reality.

Wait. Wait! Courtney Jane Salinger, what the hell are you doing?

The voice in my head is so shrill, I unclasp my hands from the back of his neck and slide them to his shoulders, pushing him away.

"Wait..." I clear my throat. "Wait. Josh, wait."

My words are desperate and breathy, and my chest heaves against his as I weakly try to put space between us.

He looks into my eyes, refusing to release me. "I want this. I want you."

But for how long? that insistent voice demands.

"Please," I say, flattening my hands on his chest. "Let me go."

His arms loosen. His eyes search mine. "What? What just happened? Court, I *want* this. I want *you*."

I want you too.

I step away, feeling confused and frustrated. "I—I know, but I don't...I mean, I don't know if this—if this is right for me."

He backhands his mouth as if trying to wipe away our kiss. "*Right for you?* What the fuck does that mean? *You* just kissed *me*."

"I know I did. I'm sorry."

My purse and laptop bag slipped off my shoulder while we were kissing, and I lean down to pick them up off the pavement.

"Don't be sorry," he says, putting his hands on his hips.

"Just—just talk to me."

He is so incredibly beautiful, and he's come to mean so much to me over the past few weeks. But I am really close to making my dreams come true. I can't let him—or anyone else—derail me now.

"I have never lied to you, Josh. I want to get married. You know that."

"So do I...*someday.*"

"No," I say, clenching my jaw and telling myself to be brave. "Not *someday*. Now. I want it now."

"Damn it, you're stubborn!" He runs a hand through his hair. "Courtney, be reasonable. Come on. Give us a chance. Give *this* a chance."

"I can't."

"Tell me you don't care about me!" He steps forward and cups my face with his hands. They're big and so warm against my cold skin, and I want to close my eyes and lean into them, lean into him, forever. He feathers a kiss on my forehead, and his voice is soft and gentle by my temple. "Tell me, baby. Tell me you don't care."

"I...can't," I admit, because I *do*. "I *do* care about you."

He kisses my forehead again, and tears fill my eyes because his touch is so reverent, so tender, it makes me want to stay like this forever. But forever isn't being offered. With all the strength I have, I force myself to step back, away from his oh-so-temporary warmth and sweetness. "Please."

"Please...*what?*" He crosses his arms, his face hardening. "Is it because I'm a *bartender*? Because I'm a—a *struggling* playwright? Because I don't make a decent living and have a posh apartment to offer you?"

I gasp as indignation rises up like spitting lava inside of me.

"Don't be an asshole, Josh. I have *never* looked down on you. You *know* that." I swipe at an escaping tear. "But the one thing I want—the *only* thing I want—is marriage, is a forever commitment. And you can think I'm crazy or stubborn or unreasonable or anything else, but you knew, *from the beginning*, what I wanted." I gulp softly and muster the last of my courage, because for me to walk away without regrets, I need to ask him one question: "Are you ready to offer me that?"

He stands there on the sidewalk across from me, his arms still crossed over his chest, and his eyes searing into mine. He licks his bottom lip and bites it, looking away from me for a second before sighing.

"No," he whispers, the sound small and strangled.

Gutted but not surprised, I heft my bags higher on my shoulder. "I didn't think so."

"Fuck! Courtney, come on! There's something here! Why can't you give us a little time to figure out what it is?"

"How much time?" I shoot back.

"What?"

"How much time? A year? Two? Three? Five? Ten?" I quit blinking back my tears and just let them fall freely. "When might you be ready for forever?"

He shakes his head and sighs again, uncrossing his arms and letting them fall at his sides. On one wrist, he wears a braided leather bracelet, and I know it's warm from his skin, and oh my God, all I want is to touch that wrist and feel that warm leather under my fingers. I'm jealous of that small scrap of leather. I'm jealous it gets to spend all day, every day, pressed against this man, flush against his skin.

"I don't know," he mutters.

His voice snaps me back to reality, and my glistening eyes meet his.

"That's why, Josh. That's why I can't give this time. Because I don't know how much time you need, and neither do you."

"So that's it?"

"That's it," I say, sniffling. My lip quivers when I add, "Be h-happy. I want you to have the b-best life ever. Just…" I clear my throat. "Just leave me alone, okay? Please, Josh. Please just leave me alone."

He doesn't say anything. He just stares at me with the same frustrated, confused, angry feelings I share with him until I can't bear it anymore. I turn away and start walking home, but I won't lie: I'm listening for his feet behind me. Part of me is praying that he'll call my name, that he'll offer me something I can accept.

But he doesn't follow me.

He doesn't call my name.

He offers me nothing.

He lets me go.

When I get home, I take my phone out of my pocket and pull up a text box, then type in "Walter DeWitt."

The message I send reads as follows:

Walter, I'm happy to accept your offer.

I will leave for London tomorrow night.
Thank you for the opportunity.
Courtney J. Salinger

CHAPTER 10

Josh

The first thing I think when I open my eyes the next morning:

She kissed me.

She kissed me, and I kissed her back, and it was the best kiss I have ever had in my entire life.

The second thing I think:

And then you let her walk away.

Fuck. FUCK!

But *of course* I let her walk away.

What other choice did I have? Marriage?

No. No way. Come on. That's nuts.

We don't know each other well enough for *marriage*. Besides, I can't support a wife. I'm not ready to be a husband or—or pay a mortgage. What about health insurance? What about a house? I can't afford my own apartment, let alone one we could share.

My head starts to ache because, fuck me, I can't offer her *anything*. Not to mention, this whole scheme makes her unreasonable, irrational, and crazy, so I shouldn't want to be with her anyway. Right? Right.

Except, no.

Wrong.

In spite of everything, I've fallen for her. Hard. At maximum, smash-your-body-on-the-pavement-below velocity.

My mind has seized on her, fixed on her, and there's nothing I can do to stop the fierce hammering of my heart when I think of her. She's what I want, and after last night's unexpected and scorching-hot kiss, I want her more than ever.

I *also* want to bellow with frustration and yell every curse word I ever learned, but Mike's sleeping in his bed on the other side of our tiny room, and it wouldn't be fair to wake him up, since he probably only got home a few hours ago.

I pick up my phone from the fruit-crate-cum-nightstand beside my bed and open a text box.

Courtney, we need to talk. I'm free today. Text me.

I stare at the message for a second, making sure it sends, then put my phone down and stretch. Looks sunny outside. I think I'll take a long run and then come back and shower. Maybe she'll have texted me back by then.

Except she doesn't.

Not on Saturday morning, or Sunday morning, or Monday morning when I wake up and check my phone first thing. By then, I've sent six messages about us talking about what happened on Friday night and haven't heard as much as a peep from her.

My desire to talk to her grows proportionately to the

amount of time I've waited, and by Monday night, driven to near madness by her silence, I leave her a rambling voice mail after several beers, asking her to please call me back. But she doesn't, and I eventually fall asleep with my phone on my chest.

The next morning, I can barely think about anything else. I'm sitting in a studio at the New Dramatists, where I'm supposed to be writing, but all I'm doing is rereading the same line of dialogue over and over again, wondering why Courtney won't talk to me. Finally, I snap. I *need* some kind of resolution, and I'm finished with her icing me out. If she won't pick up her cell or text me back, she leaves me no choice but to call her at work.

I open an internet browser and search "financial companies New York Courtney Salinger" and am gratified when a name I recognize—DeWitt, Morris & Jones—comes up. I close the door to my writing studio and dial the number, waiting a moment until the call is answered.

"Good afternoon. DeWitt, Morris & Jones. How may I direct your call?"

"Hi. I'd like to speak with Courtney Salinger, please."

"Ringing Miss Salinger's line. Hold please."

A moment later, another woman's voice answers. "Courtney Salinger's office. This is Pam speaking."

"H-Hi." I didn't expect an assistant to run interference between me and Courtney, but I also don't have a plan, so I clear my throat and say, "I'd like to speak with Courtney, please."

"Miss Salinger is not in the office at present. May I take

a message?"

Fuck. Has the assistant been warned to give unknown male callers the runaround? Hmm.

"Can you tell me when she'll be back? It's important that I speak to her." I manage to say this in a cool, collected voice.

"Miss Salinger is away on business, sir, but I am more than happy to forward a message to her."

"A-Away? When did she leave?"

"Sir?"

"I mean, I didn't know she was away."

But already I feel my muscles relaxing and my mind easing. *That's* why she hasn't texted me back or called. She's away on business. She could be anywhere. Maybe she doesn't have cell service. Either way, she's probably busy and waiting to get in touch with me when she returns.

"Sir? Did you want to leave a message?"

"Um. No. No, thank you. I'll…I'll just leave a message on her cell." *Or seven.*

"Fine. Will there be anything else?"

"No. Thank you for your help. Good-bye."

"Bye."

I press "End" on my phone and place it on my desk, sitting back in my chair.

She didn't mention that she was going out of town, but for all I know, she goes out of town for a few days every other week. How *would* I know? It's not exactly something we talked about while yelling at each other on the pavement outside of Tidewaters.

I can't help wondering where she is, and I have a fleeting notion to call her assistant back and ask or call Dina to find out more. But half a dozen texts, a rambling phone message, and a call to her office today already has me looking like a stalker. I decide to practice patience and hope she'll show up at Tidewaters on Friday.

In the meantime, I think about *why* it's so urgent that I speak to her.

I mean, we're sort of deadlocked, so what is it I want to say?

I stare at my bedroom ceiling on Wednesday night, having a conversation with myself.

What do you want, Josh? What will you say to her when you finally talk?

First and foremost, I want to convince her not to get arranged. I want to convince her that we deserve more time.

So, how do you plan to do that?

This is a sticky question because she's adamant that she (1) doesn't want to waste her time on a relationship that goes nowhere and (2) wants a solid commitment. Honestly, I don't see her giving me, and us, a chance if I don't give in a little.

I think about what commitment I'd be comfortable making to this woman right now. How far am I willing to go? How much can I stretch myself without feeling panic or pain?

I could definitely offer her exclusivity. Hell, I haven't looked at another woman in weeks anyway, so that's an easy one. And—*gulp, this is a big one*—I've never lived with anyone, but I'd take a chance jumping to cohabitation if that would make her feel more secure about my intentions. Living together. Some people don't do that for months, and I imagine it would be pretty awkward in the beginning, but if it would help her see that I'm serious about her, I'd be open to it.

It surprises me to learn that I wouldn't necessarily mind fast-tracking some of the normal steps in a relationship. After all, we've already dated and kissed. I've met her parents. Seen in a certain light, we've already been moving pretty quick. And even if a step like moving in together felt like "moving too fast," I could figure out how to adjust. After all, it's what she wants, and half of being in a relationship is meeting the other person's needs and wants. I can do that for her. She's worth it. And I know she cares about me too. She admitted it. Surely a reasonable compromise is in the cards for us.

But that night, I dream of Courtney on her wedding day.

She's wearing a white gown, but when her father lifts the veil, I'm looking through her eyes…at total and complete stranger. He's tall and blond—a cross between a tan California surfer and an ax-toting Swede. He's huge and built in ways my stocky Irish blood can barely fathom.

"Courtney Jane Salinger, I'd like for you to meet your husband, Sven Ragnar Torgersson, who is a certified millionaire with several houses, a booming financial career, and powerfully potent seed that will give you many strong sons and beautiful daughters."

*Sven winks at Courtney…*and I wake up in a cold sweat,

screaming, "No!"

"What the fuck, man?" demands Mike, throwing a pillow at me from across our dark bedroom. "Shut up! Christ!"

"Sorry," I mumble, thoughts of Sven's "powerfully potent seed" making me shake with fury and fear. The idea of *my* Courtney having sex with Sven is almost unbearable.

I pull on sweat pants and a sweatshirt and go up to the roof of our apartment building, looking out over our neighborhood and then up at the orange-hued sky.

Where are you? I wonder. *And when we meet again, will it already be too late?*

She said good-bye to me. For all I know, her match has been made.

I haven't prayed in a long, long time. Not since I left home, really. But I close my eyes and clasp my hands together, asking God to help me find a way to be with Courtney.

Amen.

***

Friday night is a disappointment.

A big, fat disappointment.

All night, I flick my eyes to the door, waiting for Dina and Courtney to breeze in together. Hoping she'll tell me that she got my messages but wanted us to have a chance to cool down before talking in person.

But she doesn't breeze in. Not her, and not Dina.

Until almost two o'clock in the morning.

I'm in a foul mood, wiping down the bar, when I hear

someone at the end of the bar ask for a beer.

"Who do I have to screw around here to get an Amstel?"

My eyes snap up, landing on Dina, who's sitting at the bar with her elbows on the counter. And no, she's not the woman I want to see, but she's the next best thing.

"Hot Stuff," I say, hoping to get some information about Courtney.

"Dumbass," she replies.

I open an Amstel and place it on a cocktail napkin in front of her.

"What do I owe you?"

"No charge," I say. "Where is she?"

"London," says Dina, lifting the bottle to take a swig.

"For how long?"

She puts the bottle down and sighs. "A month."

"Wait. What? A *month*?"

"Dumbass," she says again, taking another gulp of beer. "She's been *transferred* to London for the next four weeks. You know what that means, don't you? It means she's going to get her match while she's there."

I'm not stupid. That was the first thing that occurred to me when Dina said *A month*.

"Fuck!" I yell, putting my hands on my head and lacing my fingers together. "Fuck, fuck, fuck!"

"Indeed," says Dina, nodding at me. "You are, indeed, fucked."

"Why did she...I mean, when—"

"She left on Saturday."

The day after our fight.

"And she won't be back—"

Dina shrugs. "Mid-June at the earliest."

"She's being matched by June first," I murmur, feeling like the rug's been ripped out from under me and not liking the feeling at all.

"I know." Dina points to a neat stack of shot glasses. "I'm losing my buzz. Pour us two Tito's, huh?"

"I'm not in the mood," I growl.

"Huh. Okay. Then I'll just go home."

"No! No, no, no! Fine. I'll drink with you." I pour two shots of vodka and nudge hers the short way across the bar. "What are we drinking to?"

"Hail Marys." She picks up her glass and taps it against mine before shooting it back. "Long pass. Made in desperation. Little to no chance of success. But the clock's running down, and there's no time for anything more strategic or elegant."

"You like football?"

"I *love* football," she purrs. "Part of the reason my mummy can't find me a man is that they all love cricket more than American football."

"I can't offer her marriage," I hear myself say. "I'm not ready to get married."

"Who *is*?" she asks. "Nobody, that's who."

"Are you in touch with her?" I ask. Dina nods. "Tell her we can be exclusive. We can even move in together. I'm open to compromise."

"That would be awesome if she was too."

"But she's not."

"You know she's not." Dina shakes her head. "The girl is getting married. She's got it in her head that it's the only way for her to be happy."

"It's fucking ridiculous," I mutter.

"If you're so open to compromise, why don't you just go ahead and marry her? If it doesn't work out, get a divorce."

I think of my parents, who've been married for almost thirty years, and how terribly disappointed they would be to watch their son's marriage fail. "I don't want to get a divorce. Besides, that's crazy."

"It's not so crazy," says Dina, gesturing to the Tito's bottle. I pour us both another shot. "You'd get all the time you need to figure out if she's the girl for you, and she'd get the commitment she wants so badly."

"It doesn't work like that! Marriage isn't some crazy experiment. It's a *forever* commitment. It's for people who've dated for a few years and live together and have shared friends and a plan for their lives. I don't have a house or a— a solid job, health insurance. I don't know if she wants kids someday. Jesus, I'm a bartender, Dina. That's not the sort of—"

"You do understand the concept of arranged marriage? She's marrying a *stranger*, Josh. He could be anyone. A bartender. A gambler. Just your regular, run-of-the-mill asshole."

"The experts vet the contenders."

"Sure. But everyone lies a little."

"Dina, I'm not—"

"Besides, I don't remember her asking for health insurance and houses. She just wants someone who wants to try building something with her. And call me crazy, but I think that someone could be you."

I shake my head. "It won't work."

"How do you know that? Maybe it's the Indian in me," she says, holding up the shot glass to clink again, "but I know marriages built on a lot less can work. I've seen it. I know it's true. Hope. Optimism. Friendship. A willingness to grow together, to learn about each other, to have each other's backs. You guys already have that stuff—and heck, Josh, you and Courtney have *actual, physical attraction* too. That's a huge bonus! No matter how you look at it, getting married is a giant crapshoot. Fifty percent end in divorce, despite best intentions." She gives me a look and throws back her shot. "Oh! Wait. I take that back. *Here* fifty percent end in divorce. In *India*, where many marriages are still *arranged* and failure is not an option, the divorce rate is *one* percent."

"Are you *actually* suggesting that I marry her?" I ask, taking the bottle and putting Tito back in his place.

"I'm saying that you and Courtney already have a lot of the right ingredients for success. Would it be conventional? No. Would it be risky? Sure. Would you have to make up a lot as you went along? Yes. But who doesn't? Call me crazy, but I honestly believe you could make it work if you wanted to. I'm just…" She takes a deep breath and sighs, looking tired and a little frustrated. "I think you two care about each other. I want to see my friends happy. That's all."

I cross my arms. "So, what's the Hail Mary?"

"You already know." Dina slides off her stool and hitches her purse up on her shoulder. "It's just a matter of how much you want to be with her."

"A lot," I whisper.

"Then do what you gotta do," she says, her dark eyes severe.

"Let me get you a cab," I say, coming around the bar to walk her out. We stand on the sidewalk side by side. "You're pushy, you know."

"Yeah," she says. "I know."

"I hope I get a front row seat when *you're* going through something like this."

"Not bloody likely that'll happen anytime soon."

"Brandon Chillar played American football, you know."

"Which is why I'm an eternal Packers fan," she answers with a chuckle.

A cab pulls up to take her home, and I stand on the curb for a long moment—until the red taillights have completely disappeared into the night, until I am left alone to make the biggest decision of my entire life.

***

On the bus ride home, I do some quick math and realize that if it's two thirty in New York, it's eight thirty in London. I dial her number, but—yet again—her voice mail picks up.

"Hey," I say, "it's Josh." I look out the window, taking a moment to think about what I want to say, and then settle on, "I think you're a coward for going to London without telling me. I wish you would have stayed in New York and talked to me. I wish you'd even talk to me from London. I just—I feel like we could figure this out together if we talked." I pause again. "And I know you said to live a happy life and let you go, but that's bullshit, Court. It's total bullshit. We care about each other. We…we *have* something here, and I'm mad at you—I'm so fucking mad at you—for going away." I swallow over the lump in my throat. "I know you're not going to pick up. And I know you're not going to call me back, so I'll…I'll just…"

I realize there's nothing more to say, so I press "End" on the phone.

She made her choice: marriage.

Now it's time for me to make mine.

If I want to be with Courtney, there's only one way to make that happen, and I might already be too late. *God, please don't let me be too late.*

When I get home, everyone's asleep, so I plug in my laptop at the kitchen counter, and type in "www.arrange_me_too.com."

"Fuck," I hiss when the page comes up.

Aside from the fact that it's brutally cheesy, I forgot about the $399 fee. That much? For an e-mail address? What the actual fuck?

If I pay $399 for this goddamned service and another $1,000 for a last-minute plane ticket across the pond, that's it. I'm tapped out. I won't make rent on June 1. It wouldn't be hard to find someone to take my room, but I'll have to move out of here, and no matter what happens with

Courtney, I'll technically be homeless.

Which means this is *the* moment.

I need to make my decision now and once I do, there's no turning back.

If I fill out this form, answering every question as best I can to be matched with Courtney, I've made my choice. I'm choosing her over everything. I'm choosing her *first*.

I'm doing something I'm not comfortable doing because it's the lesser of two evils.

It wouldn't be conventional or easy, but *being* with her might make it all worthwhile.

I sit back and picture Courtney's face—at Tidewaters, at the theater, on the train, and at the wedding. Laughing with me at the Rum House and crying on the pavement after kissing me.

I love that face, I think, feeling my own soften with tenderness.

Suddenly, I hear her voice.

"Yeah. Marriage. I'd like to skip all of this crap and cut to the chase."

"I'm not dating anymore. Ever. It's soul-crushing."

"Inside of me, I'm overwhelmed that you think so well of me."

"It will happen, Josh. I believe in you."

"I can't. I do care about you."

I close my eyes as her voice fills my head, and with it, so many happy memories of time well spent with her. When I open them again, my hand has made its way to my chest and rests flattened over my heart.

And that's the moment my decision becomes final.

I wouldn't say I'm in love with her.

I definitely wouldn't say I'm ready for marriage.

But I don't want to give up on her. I don't want to give up on us.

Not now.

Not yet.

And hopefully, God help me, not ever.

CHAPTER 11

Courtney

About two weeks after I arrive in London, I am sitting across from my aunt Lucy at an elegant table in the Palm Court at the Ritz when my phone dings.

Lucy Salinger Brown Edmonton Claridge-St. James, who is my father's older sister and just divorced from her third husband, raises a sculpted brow.

"Should you check on that, dear?"

I'm about to pull my phone from my purse and take a quick look when a server arrives with a three-tiered silver stand of delectable-looking tea sandwiches. My mouth waters.

"I'm sure it can wait," I say.

"You children and all of your modern gadgets," she says. "Do let it wait. I'm famished."

It's probably the office, and frankly, they don't deserve my attention this afternoon. I told them I'd be unavailable, and I mean to stay that way. I've been at their beck and call since I arrived in London, and this is the first chance I've had to see my aunt.

I take an open-faced sandwich decorated with radishes,

cream cheese, and dill and can't help a soft murmur of delight when I take a bite.

"Is there anything as perfect as afternoon tea at the Ritz?" Aunt Lucy asks me with a delighted grin.

I smile back at her, and it occurs to me that it's probably my first genuine smile since I set foot on British soil a fortnight ago. That thought makes a lump gather in my throat and Josh's face flash up in my mind. I feel the all-too-familiar longing tighten my chest, sharp and pinching, and take a deep breath.

"Wrong pipe?" asks Aunt Lucy.

I take a sip of tea. "No. I'm fine."

But suddenly the radish and cream cheese that was so delicious a moment ago has lost all of its appeal.

I haven't heard from Josh in a week—not since last Friday night, when he called and left a message calling me a coward, then hung up the phone midsentence, like he was giving up. Since then, I'm convinced that he *has* given up on me, and as much as I try to convince myself that it's for the best, I cannot deny that I am missing him much more than I thought I would.

Every romantic thing I see in London reminds me of Josh, and since it's the height of a beautiful spring, my heart's in a permanent state of deprivation. The rainbow of flowers at Kensington Gardens and the couples that share rowboats at Regent's Park, young families brunching at sidewalk cafés in Covent Garden and crowds exiting the evening show of *Wicked* in the West End—all I can think about is how much I would have loved to share all of this with him and how sad I am to be alone.

I lift my chin.

But not for long.

Tomorrow I should be receiving my match from ArrangeMeToo.com, and then—*hopefully*—all thoughts of Josh will start to fade until he is firmly part of my past.

"You've lost your appetite?" asks Aunt Lucy, glancing at my half-eaten sandwich.

I shake my head, clear my throat, and pop the second half into my mouth.

"So, darling niece, it's been too long. I need an update on everything in the world of Courtney Jane!"

"What do you want to know, Aunt Lucy?"

"Boyfriend?"

"No," I say…*but hopefully soon.*

"No one? No contenders?"

"Not yet. But when there is, you'll be the first to know."

"Don't rush into anything," she advises, taking a puff pastry filled with egg salad and humming with pleasure as she consumes it in one bite.

"Aunt Lucy! You're one to give advice! You knew Uncle Roland for a handful of weeks before tying the knot."

"Roland Brown," she says, her eyes softening at the name of her first husband, "swept me off my sweet little co-ed feet. It was such a whirlwind, I can barely remember how it happened."

I can.

I begged her to tell me the story every time we visited

England when I was a child.

As a junior studying abroad, witty and wealthy Lucy Salinger met twice-her-age Roland Brown, the eighth Viscount Somers and a respected professor, at a mixer on her first evening at Oxford. He escorted her to every party and dance thereafter, and less than three months later, on the night she was supposed to return to the United States, they ran away to Gretna Green and got married.

Her parents were furious and threatened to disown her, regardless of the fact that she was now a viscountess. His parents were not at all pleased to have a young American in the family. But everyone settled down after a few months, and it turned out that Lucy and Roland were actually a pretty good match. Lucy brought energy and sparkle into his life, and Roland offered young Lucy stability and true love. The only problem was that their twenty-year age difference meant that Roland's heart attack at fifty-five left Lucy a widow in her midthirties, a few years before I was born.

"I love the story of you and Uncle Roland."

"*Uncle* Roland. You never even knew him, darling."

"Doesn't matter. The story was *so* romantic."

Her eyes dim for a moment. "He was my true love, you know. My one true love. I loved John Edmonton, and Frank Claridge-St. James was a good enough sort, I suppose, but Roland?" She sighs. "You never really get over your first love."

Out of nowhere, thoughts of Josh flood my mind and I look down, blinking at the starched pink napkin covering my lap.

"Courtney Jane?"

"I haven't fallen in love yet," I say, hoping that if some small portion of my heart has convinced itself that what I feel for Josh is love, denying it aloud will invalidate it.

"I know," she says thoughtfully. "Not in high school or college."

I shake my head. "The right guy never came along, I guess."

"You've had boyfriends, of course."

"Of course."

"Just no one special."

"No one who would have made a good match," I say firmly, grateful when the server reappears to refresh our hot water and offer us sweets.

For the rest of our tea, I direct the conversation toward my mother and father, and half an hour later, I'm hugging Aunt Lucy good-bye outside of the luxurious hotel.

"When shall we meet again?" she asks.

"Lunch this week?"

"I'll ring you for a date," she says. "And will you come out to Somer House next weekend?"

I think of Aunt Lucy's country estate and practically sigh with pleasure. "I'd love it."

"Be well until then, darling," she says, kissing me on the cheek before hailing a cab.

As I wave good-bye, my phone beeps in my bag, reminding me that I have incoming messages, and I reach for it, pressing my thumb on the bottom button and watching as my home screen comes up. I have two texts and several e-mails waiting.

As I stroll north from the Ritz to my flat in Mayfair, I tap on the texts. One is from Dina, telling me to have a Friday-evening gimlet somewhere amazing, and the other is from my mother, asking for the e-mail address of "that charming playwright." Apparently, Simi Frederick wants to reach out to Josh about staging one of his plays at her annual festival in Boston this October. I don't have his e-mail address, but I share his phone number and encourage her to call or text him, hoping that Simi's patronage might lead to something big. He deserves to be a success. I want that for him so badly.

Nearing my flat, I decide to detour through Grosvenor Park, the most American spot in London, with statues of two former presidents—Reagan and Roosevelt—guarding the small green space. I sit down on a park bench and breathe deeply. It's a lovely spring afternoon with blue sky and bright sun. Maybe, as Dina suggests, I should go find a posh bar and order a gimlet.

But first I should look through my e-mails and be certain there are no fires to put out at the office before my weekend officially begins. Opening the browser, my eyes scan the various senders and subjects—then my breath catches.

There it is. In black and white.

YOU'VE BEEN MATCHED

My neck snaps up, and I look around the park for someone with whom I can share my insane and important—*momentous*—news, but there's nobody, of course. I take a deep breath and center myself.

You're about to meet your husband. Your husband, *Courtney. Are you ready?*

Barely able to contain the mix of excitement, impatience, and jitters that's rolling my stomach and threatening to spill radish sandwiches all over the pristine sidewalk at Grosvenor Park, I tap on the message.

Dear Ms. Salinger:

We are excited to tell you that we have found you a match.

Meet your future husband: **CJD_NY**!

We don't believe in telling you much about your future spouse before you meet at the altar, but for your peace of mind, we can tell you that **CJD_NY** is a twenty-six-year-old male and lives in the New York, New Jersey, Connecticut tristate area. We have verified that he is currently single, has never been married, has no living children, has no criminal record, and graduated from an accredited four-year college.

When we received **CJD_NY**'s profile, something about this man spoke to our souls, and we knew that he was the right match for you. Based on our top-secret, Lifetime-backed formula for matching couples, we are excited to give you and **CJD_NY** a 90 percent chance of success.

Please remember, however, that no match will be perfect. Marriage takes an enormous amount of work, and arranged marriages take optimism and patience. That said, if you've been doing your homework, you should be prepared to enter your union with hope and readiness. Your marriage will become whatever you make it. No two matches are the same. Every couple must forge their own future together.

We will be contacting you and your match in a separate e-mail that will introduce you to one another for the first time. Please don't ask personal questions of your future spouse. You will have the rest of your life to get to know each other. This first exchange of e-mails is primarily so that you can decide on the details of your wedding. A second exchange will only be necessary to confirm those details.

We strenuously encourage you to use the services of our sister website, ArrangeMyWedding.com, to plan your big day. The experts at Arrange My Wedding will collect your birth certificates, arrange for a marriage license, and expedite any formalities in addition to reserving wedding and reception venues and planning your honeymoon. By using this service, you can keep your communication with **CJD_NY** to a minimum before you meet. These experts can plan your wedding at any time, almost anywhere in the world, and though their prices are at a premium, don't you want your special day to be perfect? A 10 percent discount for using our matchmaking service can be redeemed on your final invoice. Please use code: MARRYUS.

Although we have high hopes for you and **CJD_NY**, all marriages can hit rough patches. Should you require marriage counseling in the early days of your union, we are pleased to offer hourly rates for our personalized services in person or via Skype. It is important to us that you feel 100 percent supported in your new marriage.

We are so excited for you to begin your journey, Courtney Jane Salinger. We wish you every possible success and happiness!

With joy,

Dr. Jake, Pastor Ken, and Dr. Sydney Morningstar. Your ArrangeMeToo.com Team

CJD.

CJD.

Charles? Christopher? Christian? Colin?

I take a shaking breath, leaning back on the wooden bench and letting the late-day sun bathe my face.

Carson? Cyrus? Clifford? Chester?

I giggle softly to myself, enjoying this moment, wanting to remember it as a vital step in "The Story of Us," even though my mind is rapidly filling with more questions. I open my eyes and scan the e-mail again.

Does the "NY" at the end of his name mean he's from New York? Or is "NY" a regional tag? No "living" children…hmm. Does that mean he had a child who died? What a terrible thing, if that's true. Never married makes me feel relieved, and no criminal record is reassuring.

He's only twenty-six to my twenty-nine, but I did say that I was open to someone within five years of my age when I filled out my application. Hmm. He went to a four-year college, which means I have more education than he does, but that's okay. I requested someone with at least a bachelor's degree, and he's met that requirement.

We will be contacting you and your match in a separate e-mail that will introduce you to one another for the first time.

OMG! Does that mean…? I quickly swipe back to my inbox, and sure enough, there's another message waiting.

MEET YOUR MATCH

If my heart fluttered for the previous message, it starts hammering as I tap on this one.

Dear **CJS_NY** and **CJD_NY**:

We are delighted to introduce you to one another for the very first time.

As we shared with you in a previous message, based on our top-secret, Lifetime-backed formula for matching couples, we are excited to give your match a 90 percent chance of success. We truly believe in this process and in the potential of carefully arranged marriages to work for those in search of long-term marital happiness.

We know that you are probably very eager to meet. To that end, we ask that you exchange *a maximum of two sets of messages* in this forum as a means toward planning your wedding. *When you are ready, simply press REPLY ALL and type your message. When you press SEND*, it will come back to Arrange Me Too, and we will redirect it to your fiancé. Once again, please don't ask personal questions of your future spouse. You will have the rest of your lives to get to know each other. This first exchange of e-mails is primarily so that you can decide on the details of your wedding. The second should only be used as a follow-up, if needed.

As we shared in our previous e-mail, we strenuously encourage you to use the services of our sister website, ArrangeMyWedding.com, to plan your big day.

We look forward to hearing from each of you and request that **CJS_NY** write the first message. Within twenty-four hours, we request that **CJD_NY** write a reply. If this is not possible, please let us know at your earliest convenience.

With love,

Dr. Jake, Pastor Ken, and Dr. Sydney Morningstar.
Your ArrangeMeToo.com Team

OMG. Me? *Me* first? What do I write?

My hands are shaking, and I'm starting to feel a little bit light-headed.

I look up from my phone and take a deep gulp of fresh air. Across the park, the Marriott Hotel seems to beckon me, and I stand up in a daze, walking toward the massive structure. I stop by the concierge and am directed to the Luggage Room, an intimate, and very empty, bar off the lobby. Decorated in rich cherry wood with brown- and cream-colored leather seating, I can barely admire the beauty of the room, I'm so emotionally overwhelmed by the e-mails.

C from New York.

My future husband is C from New York, and right this second, he might be waiting for a message from me. It's a little after four o'clock here, which means it's a little after ten o'clock in the morning there. Ten. He's probably at work. I wonder what he does for work? Finance, like me? Advertising, perhaps? I try to broaden my mind. Maybe he's a teacher. Or a chef. A software engineer or a website developer. My God, he could be anything. And he could be staring at his computer, *right this second*, wondering about "C from New York." Just like me.

"A drink, miss?"

I look up to find an older gray-haired man standing behind the bar. He offers me a polite smile from under a bushy white mustache.

"Or do you need a moment?"

A line from another time comes back to me, even more relevant now than it was back in New York at the Rum House: *New bar, new drink.*

"Pick something for me?" I ask.

He stares at me for a moment, then nods.

And that's when I make an important decision: new bar, new drink...new *life*. *This* life. This new life with C from New York begins now. My heart clutches when I order it to bid farewell to Josh Dalton, but I can almost *feel* it comply. I admire it for the battle it's waged on his behalf, but my will is stronger than my heart, and I choose C from New York over Josh from Minnetonka. I choose a known happiness over unknown heartbreak. I choose C from New York.

A new drink appears before me and I take a sip,

marveling that it's a little bit bitter but surprisingly sweet too.

Good-bye, Josh Dalton, I tell myself.

I choose C from New York.

I choose him forever.

CHAPTER 12

Josh

Even though I have felt a weird sense of calm—weird because what I'm doing is the craziest thing I've ever done by a mile—for most of this week, I'm still jolted when I wake up to find an e-mail from ArrangeMeToo.com in my inbox on Friday morning.

YOU'VE BEEN MATCHED

I scrub my hands over my face and sit up in bed, glad to see that Mike's gone and I've got our room to myself.

I click on the message, and I can feel—literally *feel*—my eyes rolling with every sentence I read. Good God, this is not only crazy but downright cheesy. There's a snake-oil salesman vibe I get from the "encouragement" to use their "premium" wedding planning service, and the way they repeat my full name—Charles Joshua Dalton—several times in the body of the e-mail makes it feel really impersonal.

But it only takes me a second to figure out that **CJS_NY** is my **C**ourtney **J**ane **S**alinger, and the relief I feel makes me close my eyes and lean my head back for a second. I was so careful with my answers that I knew my application would lead me to her, but I didn't know if the timing would be right. I didn't know if I would be too late. The first major hurdle of this insanity—being matched with her—has been cleared, and I'm beyond relieved that she wasn't matched with someone else.

That said, the *biggest* hurdle of all—getting married—has yet to be managed.

I've run through several wedding-day scenarios in my mind over the course of the past week, but the one that I keep returning to is Courtney seeing me waiting at the altar, calling me an asshole (or worse) for ruining her plans and interfering with her life, and running. I really don't want that, but I know I need to prepare myself for it either way.

A second message is also waiting, this one entitled "**MEET YOUR MATCH**." Yet another hammy, impersonal introduction, this one tells me that Courtney is twenty-nine years old, has a master's degree, works in finance, was raised in New York City or its suburbs, lives on her own, and is blonde, all of which were nonnegotiable requirements on my application. It also encourages Courtney to write to me with wedding plans, and I click back to my inbox, feeling a little disappointed to discover she hasn't yet.

A knock on my door makes me look up from what I'm doing. "Yeah? Come in."

Sammy peeks in. "Hey, stranger. Can we talk?"

I pull the comforter up to my waist and close my laptop. "Sure."

She comes into the room avoiding my eyes. Sitting down on the bed beside me, I hear her take a deep breath and let it go before asking, "So, you're really doing this?"

"What? Moving out or getting married?"

"You *better* be moving out," she says. "Jenna's friend Mia is moving in on Sunday night."

Because Mia isn't taking over the couch until Sunday, my roommates said I could sleep on it tonight and tomorrow night, for which I'm grateful. More money saved to finance my time in London.

"My flight leaves on Sunday night at eight," I say. "I'll be in London on Monday morning."

"Where are you staying?"

"The Strand," I say, a hostel in the theater district that's well known by struggling actors, singers, and playwrights.

"The choice of all wandering poets," she says. "They have no elevator. Try to get a room on the lower floor."

"Good tip."

"And the…wedding?"

"I don't have a firm date yet, but soon."

Sammy nods, her eyes concerned as they hold mine. "Hmm. This is pretty nuts, Josh."

"Which part?"

"Take your pick," she says. "Moving out of your apartment. Flying to London on a whim. *Getting married to someone you barely know.*" Her eyes bug out meaningfully when she gets to that last part.

When I told Sammy, Max, Matt, and Jenna my plans, Max and Matt told me I was crazy, and Jenna wished me luck before rushing off to tell her friend that there was now a space available in our apartment. Sammy reserved judgment, saying nothing for a day or two before meeting me on the roof with two beers on Wednesday night. Her comments were sparse but disapproving, and we ended our conversation when I got angry and walked away.

"Max and I have been together for years," she notes. "And we haven't even *talked* about getting married. I didn't—I mean, I didn't even know you were looking for a wife."

"I wasn't."

"Then…?"

"I wasn't looking for marriage, but I happened to fall for someone who is."

"You're so fucking impulsive when it comes to women!"

She's right, *and* she'd know. When I first pursued Sammy, it was a little like this. I wanted her bad, and I didn't back off until we were together. It just turned out we were better as friends than lovers in the end.

"When I find what I want, I go for it."

"Well, the whole thing is just insane," she says.

"I know it *sounds* that way, but it's what she wants." I think about Courtney, about how much I've missed her these past two weeks, and about how my mind and heart have undergone a certain transformation. I don't know if I "believe" in arranged marriage. I don't know if it'll work out any better than a traditional American courtship, engagement, and marriage. But I can't bear the thought of her with someone else, and my feelings for her are genuine, so I've decided to take a leap. "*For her*, I'm willing to try."

"I can't change your mind?" Sammy asks me, reaching

out to wrap her fingers around my forearm.

"Nah. I'm already in. It's too late."

Her fingers brush my arm. "Do you love her, Josh?"

I think about this for a second. I've asked myself the same question many times over the past few weeks, and the honest answer is "I don't know."

"Running off to London to marry her makes a good case that you do." I don't say anything, so she continues, "I just—I wish you could take your time, you know? Date for a while. Even for a couple of months. Make sure it's right before you get all tangled up with someone you barely know."

"I'm already tangled, Sam."

"I guess you are," she says, sliding her hand from my arm. "If it doesn't work out—"

"Don't do that."

"*If it doesn't work out*," she says again, her brown eyes focused like lasers on mine, "come home."

I grin at her. "I don't live here anymore."

"We'll figure it out," she says, biting her bottom lip for a second before releasing it.

For a split second, I feel like I might be picking up on a vibe from her, but the moment passes. Besides, she's with Max, and our short-lived love affair was a long time ago. I decide I'm just imagining things.

"Thanks, Sam."

She nods, then gets up from my bed. When she gets to the door, she turns around. "I'd tell you not to do anything stupid, but…" She shrugs. "Have a safe trip, okay?"

"Okay."

The door closes behind her, and it occurs to me that Sammy and Dina are coming from exact opposite places where this whole marriage thing is concerned. Dina's all like *Take a chance. Your odds are good*, while Sam can barely discuss it without calling me impulsive and insane. I guess my own opinion falls somewhere in the middle. Yeah, it's impulsive. Yeah, it's insane. But I'm taking a chance and hoping my odds are good.

My laptop dings, and I open it up.

MESSAGE #1 FOR CJD_NY FROM CJS_NY

I take a deep breath and tap on the message, ignoring the stupid fourteen-year-old girl butterflies in my stomach.

Dear CJD_NY:

I've been staring at my screen for ten minutes trying to figure out what to say to you. Nothing sounds exactly right, so I decided to start with telling you how I feel: excited and nervous. Grateful that you decided to apply for this process and hopeful that our marriage will be long and happy, even though it's happening in a really unconventional way.

I want you to know that I am 100 percent committed to this process. I trust it. I believe in it. I want it to work, and when I set my mind to something, I rarely give up. When I meet you and take my vows, I'll mean every word.

My life took a bit of an unexpected detour two weeks ago, and although I live in New York, I'm working in London for the next two weeks. If you are interested in getting married in London, I'm happy to take care of all planning expenses on this end, as long as you can get yourself here for the wedding by June 15. If you would prefer to get married in New York, we can plan for June 22. It's up to you.

I'm scared, CJD_NY, but I was scared the first time I tried riding a bike, or driving a car, or applying to college, or skydiving (I only did that once!). But I figure it's going to be you and me against the world, and as long as you believe in this process and agree that arranged marriages can work with patience, persistence, and mutual respect, I know that we can make it too.

Huge thanks to Dr. Jake, Pastor Ken, and Dr. Sydney Morningstar. I hope that my husband and I will have a chance to thank you in person one day soon.

With hope and joy,

CJS_NY

It's *so* Courtney.

So, so, so Courtney, I can hear her saying these words, and it makes me feel strong and protective. What if she'd been matched with someone else and some other guys was reading these precious words right now? It makes me want to punch something and thank someone at the same time.

Thank God for Dina's push last weekend and for her interference in general. She helped fast-track me to the place where I need to be today, and I'm grateful to her.

Like Courtney, there's a part of me that's scared to

death, but also like Courtney, I'm getting to a place where even if I hate these "experts" and this "process," I'm committed to *her*. Part of me is terrified to think of Courtney as my wife, but there's a stronger part of me that's growing to love the idea too. When I say my vows to her on June 15, just like her, I'll mean them. And as best as I can, I'll live up to them.

So many feelings are bubbling up inside of me, I figure I may as well write her back now and let those emotions drive my words.

Dear CJS_NY:

I know what you mean. This is really unconventional, but I guess we both have our reasons for choosing this path. Maybe our reasons are really different, but we'll have the rest of our lives to figure out "the why of everything" together.

When I say "I do," I'll mean it, and I'm going to do everything I can to make you happy. Let's make a promise that whomever we see at the altar, we'll still go through with this, okay? I'm not covered in warts or scars or anything like that, but I just want to be sure that we're both committed to each other and this crazy journey—no matter what. Can you give me your promise?

Turns out that London is one of my favorite cities, and I have a little vacation time coming up. I choose to marry you on June 15 in England. Just tell me where to be.

I'll be the one in the penguin suit.

With affection,

CJD_NY

I read it, reread it, make a couple of small edits, and then hit "Send."

Once I do, I'm so jittery with a mixture of nerves and excitement, I pull on some shorts and a T-shirt. I have just enough time to take a run and have lunch before heading to Tidewaters for my final shift.

***

When I told Lulu and Harvey that I needed to take off the month of June, they weren't too happy, but Lulu said that as long as I walked back in the door by June 30, I could have my job back. The thing is, I have no idea what my life will look like by the end of June. The *only* thing I know is that I'll be married to Courtney by then. Still, I'm really grateful to know that the option's open if I need it.

Annie pinches me on the ass when she arrives for her shift at three o'clock.

"What's this I hear about you taking a month off?"

The bar's quiet, so I'm wiping down glasses that have just come out of the dishwasher. "Yep. Headed to London tomorrow."

"For your playwriting?"

Among other things. "Yeah. I hope to do some writing over the next couple of weeks."

"You're abandoning me, Joshua."

"Never. I'll be back."

"Sure about that? Lulu didn't seem positive."

I lean forward and kiss her cheek. "Whether I come back to work or not, I'll come back to see you, beautiful."

She blushes. "My grandson had me up at the crack of dawn. Let's hope I can get through this shift, huh?"

"I'll stay late. You go at midnight."

"You're a prince! See? This is why I'm going to miss you, honey."

She heads to the break room to change, and I pick up my phone.

I got another message from Courtney right before I got to work, and it said two things:

Yes, she promised to marry me no matter what.

And that she'd see me on June 15 in England.

From now on, all necessary details will come from our ArrangeMyWedding coordinator, Melissa. I lean back against the bar and reread her first message, my heart swelling when I get to the part of about her fears. I wish I could walk around London holding her hand and reassuring her that everything was going to be okay. And when I get to the part about "you and me against the world," I smile to myself like a lovesick teen. Something about me and Courtney against the world just feels…good.

The front door swings open, and I look up to find Dina rushing in.

"Hey!"

"Hey!" she says, perching on a barstool. "I only have a minute. I'm leaving for JFK in, like, ten minutes."

"Oh, yeah?" I ask. "Where are you headed?"

"It's a secret," she says, winking at me.

"A secret, huh? I've never known you to be cagey about anything, Hot Stuff. You're an open book."

"Not about *everything*." She shrugs. "Can I get an Amstel or what?"

I pour a glass of beer for her and place it in front of her. "No charge."

"Why, thank you, kind sir." She looks nervous. "So, um, are *you* going anywhere? Any trips planned?"

"I'm leaving for London tomorrow."

"Yes! Phew!" Her smile splits her face. "I *knew* it. Oh, my God. Yes! I mean, when she told me she'd been arranged with someone called CJD, I might have worried for a second, but I hoped it was you!"

"Why'd you worry?"

"*C*…JD. Who's C?"

"Ohh." I nod, immediately understanding her confusion. "It's me. Charles Joshua Dalton."

"Ah-ha! There we go." She takes a drink of her beer. "I mean, what if some hot guy named Christian got the jump on you?"

I chuckle, looking up as two women sit a few stools down. They order white wine, and I give them generous pours so they'll leave me alone to chat with Dina for the few minutes she'll be here.

"Any last-minute advice?" I ask her.

"She's gonna be pissed."

I wince. "You think?"

"Oh, yeah. She had a plan, and it *didn't* include you."

"She had no idea *who* it included. May as well be me."

"She'll still see it as interfering."

"Well, she promised to marry me no matter what."

"Wait. She knows it's *you*?"

"No. She promised to marry CJD. And that's me, so…how about that advice?"

"Relax your jaw before she gets to the altar," says Dina, looking at me over the rim of her pint glass.

"Why?"

"So that it won't hurt so bad when she punches you in the face."

"Did anyone ever tell you that you suck at pep talks?"

"Aw. And see, I was sort of patting myself on the back for playing Cupid so well."

I flatten my hands on the bar between us and look square into her dark eyes. "I can't thank you enough, Dina. Seriously. You pat your back as much as you want. Just be careful of your wings."

She places her hand over her heart and pretends to swoon. "And just think, if I'd made my move, you'd be all mine by now."

I grin at her. "Nah. We wouldn't have worked out."

"We might've," she teases. "For one night. In a very dark room."

"Bad girl," I say.

"Always," she promises, finishing off her beer. She wipes her lips and gives me a smile. "Wish me luck?"

"You don't need it."

"Do it anyway."

I offer her my hand.

"Good luck, Dina," I say.

"Good luck, Josh," she answers. "Be good to my best friend or you'll have to relax your balls too."

I bust out laughing, and she slides her hand away, waving over her shoulder as she breezes out of Tidewaters and slips into the town car waiting for her by the curb.

CHAPTER 13

<u>Courtney</u>

If I thought that Aunt Lucy was going to be supportive of my married-at-first-sight plan in light of her very short courtship with Uncle Roland, then I was sorely mistaken. Sorely as in *completely*.

The first thing she asks me is, "Do your parents know about this—this *scheme*?"

"Not yet. I thought that maybe we could—"

"We? *We?* No, no, no. Absolutely not! I'm not—my God, what are you doing? What are you *thinking?* Why are you doing this? This is ridiculous, Courtney Jane! Insanity! Dangerous!" she shrieks at me, becoming increasingly more hysterical. "I'm calling my brother! No! First, I'm calling Dr. Phillips to come out for a home visit. You need to see someone! To—to talk to someone! You need help! With your head!"

She bustles off to find her psychiatrist's phone number, muttering under her breath about her insane niece, and I stand in the front hall of her country estate and let my duffel bag fall with a light thud to the white marble floor.

"Miss Salinger," says her butler, who appears discreetly

out of nowhere. "May I take your bag upstairs?"

"Thank you, Earnest," I say. "The pink room?"

"Your aunt insisted that we prepare it for you."

Aunt Lucy decorated one of her guest rooms in fuchsia to celebrate my first visit to England almost twenty years ago, and even though it feels a little "sparkalicious" for my adult self, I never stay anywhere else when I visit.

I climb the familiar stairs, wondering what it was about my news that set her off so thoroughly.

"Hi, Aunt Lucy."

"Hello, darling."

"Thanks so much for having me stay."

"I couldn't be more delighted!"

"I have news…"

"Tell me!"

"I'm getting married!"

"W-What?"

She stood there staring at me, so I gave her an overview of the Arrange Me Too process and told her that I'd been matched and that I planned to be married in two weeks. When she didn't say anything, I asked for the name of the hotel in Gretna Green where she and Uncle Roland tied the knot so I could book it. I guess that jolted her out of her state of shock, because that's when she started yelling at me.

I'm halfway up the stairs when she calls from the vestibule, "Dr. Phillips will be here at four o'clock. I'm paying him triple to drive up from London, so you best be ready to meet with him. Do you hear me, miss?"

I hear her, and if it makes her feel better, I'll talk to her shrink, but my mind is made up, and nothing he says is going to change it at this point.

"That's fine."

She follows me up the stairs. "Darling, I'm—I'm sorry I yelled, but I'm *worried* for you. I'm *concerned*. I've never *heard* of anything like this."

When I reach the landing, I turn around and give her a dry look. "That's a bit of an exaggeration. Arranged marriage is a common practice in many countries."

"Not *this* one!" she bellows. "And not *yours*!"

"Aunt Lucy," I say, placing my hands gently on her shoulders. "It's happening in two weeks. I'm getting married in *two weeks*. No matter what."

She crosses her arms over her ample bosom. "We'll just see about that."

Two hours later, her psychiatrist arrives from London, and the three of us sit together in her living room to discuss my descent into madness.

Aunt Lucy sniffles. "I'm afraid she's having a nervous breakdown."

Dr. Phillips, who is in his sixties with gray hair and horn-rimmed glasses, raises his bushy eyebrows at me. "Are you having a nervous breakdown, Courtney?"

"No. I just don't want to date anymore. I want to get married."

He asks me to share the story behind my decision, and I tell him about my abysmal dating life, my fears of never finding happiness, and my decision six weeks ago to be arranged by expert. At his request, I bring down my laptop and show them both the matchmaking website and e-mails. When I have finished answering all of their questions as thoughtfully as possible, I sit back on the couch and wait for Dr. Phillips' diagnoses.

"Well?" says Aunt Lucy, worrying a Kleenex in her hand.

"You may not *like* her decision, Lucy," says Dr. Phillips, "or *agree* with it, but in my opinion, your niece's mind is sound. She has chosen an uncommon method of finding a spouse, but I think she's been mindful and deliberate in making her choice." He pauses, then looks over at me. "I cannot imagine this was a popular decision with your parents either. What feedback did they give you?"

"I only met my match yesterday." I take a deep breath and hold it for a minute, feeling like I'm back in grade school when I grudgingly admit, "I haven't told them yet."

He lifts his chin and stares at me extra hard. "You need to tell them."

"I will." *Eventually.*

"Within the week," he says. "Before the ceremony."

I don't mean to roll my eyes, but I do, because if my aunt overreacted, my parents will absolutely, positively *Lose. Their. Shit* over this.

"Why?" I ask him. "They'll just be awful and try to talk me out of it."

"You don't know that," he says. "What if they want to come? What if they're hurt that they weren't invited? What if it causes a rift that could have been avoided?"

"They won't want to come. They'll be as upset as Aunt

Lucy. Even more." My aunt is sobbing softly beside me, which I hate because it kills me to hurt her, so I put my arm around her shoulder and pull her closer. "Once they come to terms with it, they could host a reception at their country club to introduce C to their friends as my new husband."

"Courtney, I'm here to give you my honest and professional guidance, and I don't agree with—"

"They'll try to stop it," I say in a rush. For the first time since our conversation began, my eyes fill with tears, and I blink at Dr. Phillips. "They're wealthy and connected, and they'll—they'll do everything they can to stop it. I know it."

My aunt pipes up. "You don't know that—"

"Aunt Lucy," I say, "why did you elope with Uncle Roland? Why did you go to Gretna Green? Why didn't you go home to Connecticut and get married?"

She takes a deep, sobby breath and reaches up to dry her cheeks with her soaked tissue. "Please, darling, that situation was completely diff—"

"*Why* did you elope?" I ask again, this time with an edge in my voice.

"Because…" she starts. She clears her throat. "Well. Roland was quite a bit older than me, and we'd only known each other for a few months when we—"

"*Please*, Aunt Lucy," I beg her. "Tell the truth."

"Oh, fine." She exhales loudly, grumbling at me. "Because my father and brother would have tried to stop me…us. They *never* would have gone along with it."

"Your brother," I say. "Who is also…my father."

She nods. "Yes."

"Your father is controlling?" asks Dr. Phillips.

"He loves me," I explain, "but I'm his only child. I've tried very hard to live up to his expectations, to live my life in a way that would make him proud. But…but I don't want to date some prep-school guy who still funnels beers at parties, has a junior golf membership at Waveny, and knows everyone I know and marries me because I'm an appropriate choice from a good family. I just want someone who matches *me*. Someone chosen especially for *me*. Someone who's the right match for *me*." I squeeze my aunt's shoulder. "Like Lucy and Roland."

"I understand," whispers Lucy, sniffling as she leans her head against my shoulder. "I understand, darling."

"I'm not crazy," I say.

"I know," she says.

"I want this."

"I can see that."

"I'll tell my parents when it's done. I promise."

I feel her flex her jaw against my shoulder, but she doesn't argue.

"Well, that's that. I think my work here is done," says Dr. Phillips. He reaches for the briefcase at his feet. "I'll bill you, Lucy?"

She stands up and gives him a hug. "Thanks for driving up."

"My godson's at Milton Keynes. Thought I might continue up and surprise him with dinner tonight."

"How nice," says Lucy. "We won't keep you any longer."

I stand up and offer my hand to Dr. Phillips. "Thanks for helping us sort things."

"You're an unusual young woman," he says, shaking my hand. "I wish you all possible luck, Miss Salinger. I hope everything works out as you hope."

"Me too," I say, sitting back down on the sofa as my aunt walks him to the front hall.

When she returns to the room a few minutes later, Earnest follows her, carrying a silver tray with two champagne flutes and a bottle of wine on ice.

"I guess we should toast your—your joy," says Aunt Lucy, her tone lackluster.

"I'd love that," I say, standing up to put my arms around her and kiss her cheek with gusto. "And then…how about you tell me all about Gretna Green?"

***

It takes two hours on Sunday to fill out the dozens of forms for my planner, Melissa, from ArrangeMyWedding.com, but it's so exciting, I'm smiling at my laptop the entire time.

Their "premium" price is exorbitant, but my savings account is ample, ready, and waiting. I will spare no expense to get exactly what I want on extremely short notice.

I tell Melissa that C and I want to be married on Saturday, June 15, at the Old Gretna Parish Church, with a small supper to follow at Gretna Hall for me, C, and Aunt Lucy. I ask for white and peach roses in my bouquet, a calla lily boutonniere for C, simple gold bands, a minister of any protestant denomination to perform the service, and Pachelbel's "Canon in D" to play as I walk down the aisle.

I choose the traditional Scottish vows, which include the words "With my body, I thee worship, and with all my worldly goods, I thee endow."

I won't lie, a shiver goes down my spine when I think about *sharing my body* with C.

While I'm not against having sex on our wedding night if we have chemistry and an instant connection, I know the likelihood of us clicking that fast is slim. I hope he will be patient with me if I need some time to get used to him.

On the Lifetime television program, which I binge-watched on my flight over and have continued to watch during my free time in the UK, the biggest problem the arranged couples face is often a lack of chemistry. They see each other, and what they see just isn't what gets their motors revving. What if that happens with us? What if C wants someone stick-thin and brunette? What if he's some Ed Sheeran look-alike, all red and freckled, short and stocky?

I am instantly ashamed of myself.

No matter what he looks like, he will be my *husband*.

My forever.

I remind myself that physical attraction can grow out of love, which can grow out of friendship, which grows from mutual respect, common goals, and kindness. Maybe we won't have that *zing*—that je nais se quoi of immediate attraction. And maybe we won't have sex for a week or a month or a year, but when we do, it'll be because we chose each other on our wedding day and took our time falling in love.

I'm okay with that.

I'm more than okay with that.

I *can't wait* to fall in love with my husband.

When I finish entering the final details about our wedding ceremony on the web forms, I scroll to the next page, which requests the details of our honeymoon, should we wish for ArrangeMyWedding.com to plan it for us.

I consider this for a moment, thinking about the fact that I'm headed back to London tonight and I'll be up at the crack of dawn tomorrow, headed to the office. My next two weeks are spoken for, and I'll be burning the midnight oil right up until the day before the wedding, when I'll travel to Scotland with Aunt Lucy. If I want a honeymoon at all, it's probably best to hire someone else to do the planning.

But…where to go? Back to London? Over to Edinburgh?

I bite my lower lip, glancing up at the bookcase across from me that flanks a large fuchsia-cushioned window seat. My eyes land on the spine of one of my all-time favorite books, *Outlander* by Diana Gabaldon, and suddenly my fingers fly across the keys of my laptop, asking Melissa to please schedule a five-day, four-night honeymoon in the Scottish Highlands, to begin the day after the wedding.

I click "Send" before I can change my mind, then close my laptop. That's it. My planner has all of my requests and everything she should need, including a photo of my passport and—

Knock, knock.

"Come in."

Aunt Lucy peeks her head into my room. "Put your

shoes on."

"Where are we going?"

"It's a surprise."

The door closes, and I hop up to throw on a cardigan sweater and slip my feet into silver ballerina flats. I grab my purse and head downstairs to find Aunt Lucy waiting for me by the front door.

"Tell me," I say.

"Nope."

Earnest opens the door and we step outside, where Aunt Lucy's Jaguar is waiting for us. She opens her door and sits down behind the wheel as I take a seat beside her.

"Another psychiatrist?"

"Hush up," she says, leaning forward to turn on the radio.

A medley of fifties and sixties music accompanies us on our otherwise uneventful drive to the Mall in Luton.

"The Mall?" I ask, grinning at her as she enters the parking garage. "We've been here a million times. This was your big secret?"

She parks close to the entrance, and I dutifully follow her into the lift, watching as she presses the button for the Gallery.

"Are we doing some shopping, Aunt?"

"*You* are."

The elevator doors open, and she steps out, heading briskly to the left.

"Where in the world are we…"

That's when I understand.

She's stopped outside of an elegant wedding boutique. Two mannequins dressed in frothy white creations stand in the windows that flank the front door. My eyes dart from the dresses to my aunt's beloved face.

"You need a wedding dress, darling," she says simply, just as the store manager arrives to open the glass doors and welcome us into the bridal salon.

"Lucy Salinger?" she asks, shaking my aunt's hand. "Then this must be Courtney. The bride."

The *bride*.

I know I should look at boutique clerk, shake her hand, and thank her for accommodating us at the last minute, but I can't. All I can do is launch myself into my aunt's arms, murmuring my thanks as I try to keep the tears at bay.

Because for the first time since I started this entire process, I *feel* like a *bride*.

***

Two weeks fly by with days full of work and hours spent online every evening with Melissa as we finalize the details for the wedding and honeymoon together.

I pack up my London apartment, sending almost everything back to New York and only packing what I need for my wedding and honeymoon.

On Friday afternoon, Aunt Lucy picks me up at work. Before I know it, we're Scotland-bound by train, racing north on the tracks, ever closer to my wedding, to my husband, to my chosen destiny.

While Aunt Lucy sleeps across from me, I think about tomorrow—or do my best to think about it without totally freaking myself out.

It's been thirteen days since I received my one and only message from C, and if it were written on paper, it would be worn from handling by now. As it is, I have it mostly memorized.

My favorite parts are when he writes that when he says, "I do," he'll mean it and that he's going to do everything he can to make me happy. I love the promise and optimism in those words. I love the hope he has for us, because I share it.

In the first paragraph, he mentions his reasons for "doing this" might be different than mine, which has made me wonder over and over again what they might be. Like me, did he come to loathe modern dating? Or are his reasons completely different? Perhaps he isn't good at choosing the women in his life and wanted help from experts. Or perhaps he's a very busy executive and isn't able to date very often. Maybe he's just a fan of the television show. I have no idea. I don't really care, even though I probably should. But from the moment I happened upon Arrange Me Too, I've cared less about *who he is* than *what we will share*, and that hasn't changed. Whoever he is, I will marry him, and I will grow to love him. The rest, frankly, doesn't matter.

An announcement on the overhead system wrestles me from my dreamy thoughts: "Passenger Dalton, please come to the conductor's office in car four to retrieve your lost passport. Passenger Dalton."

Dalton.

The name presses against my chest and steals my breath for a second, some erstwhile feelings making my heart race, pounding in my ears as the conductor repeats the message.

Dalton. Like Josh.

Not Josh, of course. Josh is in New York.

But maybe a distant cousin from Ireland. Someone who has his dark-brown hair or bright-blue eyes or little dimple that only shows up sometimes, when something really makes him laugh.

I sit up as straight as I can and crane my neck to see if anyone stands up in our car to answer the page, but everyone stays put, and the melancholy that passes through me feels...awful.

I look out the window at the passing darkness, willing myself not to be affected by the mere mention of a familiar name, but it's futile. Though I've been distracted by living in London and planning my wedding, thoughts of Josh have lurked close to the surface, and now they're pushing up, up, up, into my consciousness, into my now.

My stomach buzzes and my eyes water.

I miss him.

God, I wish I didn't miss him.

I blink at my reflection, surprised by my sudden and intense reaction. I haven't heard from him in weeks. Certainly he's forgotten me by now. I mean, we weren't actually *together*. We weren't a couple. What's to remember?

And yet, when *I* think of *him*, my heart fists and I feel so lonely, I almost shiver from it.

For such a short-lived relationship, Josh Dalton had more of an impact on me than any other man I ever dated.

I check my watch to see it's a little after six here. He

won't be arriving at Tidewaters for hours yet, but I picture him behind the bar—the way his eyes would light up when I walked in, how he'd linger by me to talk and joke about making the "perfect" gimlet. Suddenly, I'm transported forward in time to the night we kissed on the sidewalk. *Courtney, Courtney, Courtney, I knew it would be like this…*

My fingers reach up to brush across my lips, and a soft mewling sound escapes from my throat.

Am I making a mistake?

My wedding dress is in a box over my head, plans have been made for a Scottish wedding with my arranged fiancé, and my bags are packed for a Highlands honeymoon, but— *Oh, God*—could this all be a huge mistake?

I pick up my phone and tap on a text box, bringing up Josh's name. But the longer I stare at it, the more I realize that I have nothing to say. I still want to be married. He doesn't. And that's precisely why this *isn't* a mistake.

Nevertheless, my mind flits back to our very first conversation that strange night in April, when I first told him that I was sick of the dating game and was going to figure out a way to get married. It even makes me grin, in a sad sort of way, to remember saying that to him and to think of where I am right now—literally headed to my wedding.

I type out a quick message, half closure and half bait, because for whatever reason, I am longing to hear Josh's voice again. Just one more time. One last exchange.

I'm getting married tomorrow. I just wanted you to know.

I hit "Send," then clutch my phone to my breast with white knuckles.

It buzzes a moment later.

Beautiful. Smart. Funny. Kind…and brave.

He's the luckiest guy in the world, Courtney.

The tears in my eyes spill onto my cheeks as I read and reread the simple and sweet message. It breaks my heart a little, but in its own aching way, it's perfect. It makes me *feel* brave. And gifts me unexpected peace.

Maybe it's okay if I always care for Josh Dalton just a little bit.

Maybe it's okay because he was an important part of this journey.

Because I wouldn't be getting married tomorrow if it wasn't for a conversation with Josh Dalton so many weeks ago.

Still clutching my phone to my heart, I curl up in my seat and fall asleep.

***

Saturday is a whirlwind of activity with Melissa at the helm. She is British and bossy and totally in control, which I find I love. I place myself in her competent hands, and off we go for prewedding preparations.

I'm waxed to within an inch of my life, but a full-body massage makes it all better. Aunt Lucy and I get our hair done and our nails painted. A girl from the salon comes to the Gretna Hall Hotel to do my makeup while Melissa takes my dress to be steamed, and as the wedding draws nearer, Aunt Lucy only begs me to rethink my "crazy scheme."

At four o'clock, I fasten my white strapless satin bra, pull on my matching satin-and-lace panties, and take my brand-new kitten heels from their brand-new box. Just as I ask Aunt Lucy to help me with the clasp on my pearls, there's a knock on our door.

"I'll get it," says Lucy.

She returns a moment later with a small blue box sitting atop a card-sized white envelope.

"What's that?" I ask.

"I have no idea."

"Come on. Is this from you?"

"No, darling," she says. "I promise it's not."

She hands me the box and envelope, and I open the latter, which reveals a white card with two gold wedding bands on the front and reads, "Our Wedding Day."

"It's from him!" I gasp.

"Well, read it!"

I open the card with shaking fingers.

Dear CJS:

I'm not scared anymore.

I can't wait to see you. I can't wait to marry you. I can't wait to be your husband.

Today, I'm the luckiest guy in the world.

Xoxo

The words are incredibly romantic and sweet, but there's a streak of melancholy that passes through me as I read words so similar to the ones Josh used last night to encourage me from thousands of miles away.

"That's lovely," says Aunt Lucy with a sniff, as though she's still reserving judgment on C's character. "What's in the box?"

I place the card back inside the envelope and open the box to find a ring. Decorating a simple gold band is a single emerald-cut garnet, and that's when it occurs to me: my fiancé has sent me an engagement ring. And not just an engagement ring, but a ring that bears my birthstone too.

And for a second—*just a split second*—I wonder if I might actually be the luckiest *girl* in the world.

"He's thoughtful," says Lucy, "if not a little thrifty."

"Aunt Lucy!"

"Well, it's no diamond, is it?"

I give her a dirty look before taking the ring from its velvet bed and slipping it on the fourth finger of my left hand. It fits perfectly, and I have a sudden rush of hopefulness that makes me feel almost giddy.

Melissa sweeps into the room with my dress a moment later, and she helps me get dressed as Aunt Lucy finishes her toilette in my bathroom. When she returns, I'm dressed, and she gasps with surprise, covering her mouth as tears rain down on her cheeks.

"You'll ruin your makeup!" I say, rushing to hug her despite my too-tight shoes and snug dress.

"Forget my makeup," she says, holding me close. "You look so beautiful. Like a bride."

"I *am* a bride," I say, leaning away to look into her blue eyes. "Thank you for everything. For going along with this and walking me down the aisle and not telling my mom and dad."

"I'll regret it, I'm sure."

"I'm not making a mistake," I insist.

Her eyes are sad as she releases me to find her purse.

"I hope not, because I checked on your groom, and he's already waiting for you at the church," says Melissa. "Which means it's time for us to go."

"You've done an amazing job," I say. "Thank you for everything."

She nods in her businesslike way, ushering me toward the door and calling to Aunt Lucy to meet us at the car.

On the way to the church and to calm my nerves as we wait for the ceremony to start, I think about a movie I once saw.

I think it took place in the Middle Ages…or maybe Viking times? I'm not sure, but I know one thing for certain: in the movie, there was an arranged marriage. A man loyal to the king of England, but without land or wealth, was betrothed to a woman who had both.

But he's never seen her, and she's never seen him. And in the movie, she's wearing this thick veil that keeps her face hidden.

There's no way for him to know what's behind the veil.

There's no way for him to know to whom he's about to bind his life.

A priest tells them to hold hands, and they do.

But just before she takes her vows, she reaches for her veil, and—

Ooof.

An elbow in my side brings me swiftly back to reality. I'm standing beside Aunt Lucy in the vestibule of a very old, very charming church in Gretna Green, Scotland…and I'm about to get married to a stranger.

"You don't have to do this," my aunt hisses, her breath hot on the shell of my ear. "This is craziness, Courtney. Utter insanity."

I clench my teeth together. Hard.

"I love you, Aunt Lucy, but you don't have to stay."

"I'm not leaving." She takes my hand in a death grip. "But there is absolutely no reason for you to do this! Darling, reconsider—"

"Please, Aunt Lucy," I bite out, touching the garnet ring on my left hand.

"We can turn around right now," she continues, her tone passing panic and veering into hysteria. "Run out of here. The car's waiting in the parking lot. We'll drive straight to the airport. We could just—"

"No."

I try to take a deep breath, which reminds me that I'm in a corseted white dress. I think I've been stress eating over the past two weeks because it's tight around my lungs, and I can't fill them completely.

"You can still change your mind," she insists with tears in her voice.

"No."

"*Please* don't do this," she begs me in a thin whisper.

I feel a bead of sweat start at the nape of my neck, just beneath a careful updo, and make its way down my spine, which is covered in white lace. Suddenly, at the very moment I *might* have reconsidered what I am about to do, I hear Pachelbel's "Canon in D" start playing inside the small church. Not a second later, the ancient dark-wood doors before us are whooshed open.

I gasp softly, instantly turning my gaze downward to the threadbare red carpeting that runs from the narthex to the altar.

To calm myself, I think of the man in the movie.

How many others have done the same in this very place? I wonder, taking my first step down the aisle. *Married someone they've never met before?*

One step. Another.

It probably worked out fine for them, I tell myself.

Step together. Step.

It's time, Courtney. Look up.

Step together. Step.

For God's sake, Courtney Jane! You wanted this. You chose this. Now, have courage and look up, God damn it!

Nearly halfway down the aisle, I raise my chin, but only enough to see the Presbyterian minister's cream-colored robe embroidered with gold crosses. Peripherally, to his left, I can see the form of a man.

I'll be the one in the penguin suit.

"It's not too late!" my aunt sobs softly, squeezing the blood from my hand.

In defiance of her words, I lift my head all the way.

My lips pop open.

My breath catches.

My heart stops.

OH. MY. GOD.

Josh.

JOSH?

Josh is here. WHY is Josh here?

My feet freeze, and I blink at him.

What's happening? What the hell is going on? Why is Josh is standing where my future husband should be standing?

"W-what is th-this?" I whisper, feeling light-headed. "What's h-happening?"

My bouquet slips from my fingers, and I'm dimly aware of it hitting the floor.

"Breathe, Court," he says, taking a step toward me.

But I can't.

"J-Josh...?" I sputter.

"Breathe," he orders, holding out his hand to me. "Come stand next to me. It's okay, baby."

But it's not. It's definitely not okay.

I try to take a step, or even *a breath*, but my lungs are so squished and my heart is racing so fast, I can't. Panicking, I try to inhale again, but it feels like my throat is closing. I try to speak, to explain that I can't breathe, but the room starts spinning.

I wobble. I start to fall. And then—

Blackness.

CHAPTER 14

Josh

Of all the scenarios I imagined, Courtney fainting into my arms before even reaching the altar wasn't among them. But the weight of her body in my arms feels like a sweet relief after these weeks apart. I lift her easily into the cradle of my arms and glance up at the minister.

"Where can we…?"

"Oh, aye! Right! Back here."

He leads the way to a small room behind the altar that I assume is his office, and I sit down in a comfortable leather chair, still holding my fiancée close. Truth? I have no intention of letting her go. Ever.

"Right." Melissa clears her throat. "Eh, Mr. Fitzgibbons, perhaps we should give the young people a moment?"

"Yes. Aye, of course. Right."

She ushers the clergyman back into the church, and I'm grateful for a moment alone with my bride—until I realize there's still someone in the room with us.

An older lady wearing a smart peach-colored suit approaches from the doorway and looks me over. "You're C,

I suppose?"

I nod, offering her a hand from my chair. "Charles Joshua Dalton."

She shakes it from where she's standing across from me. "Based on my niece's reaction to seeing you, I hardly need to ask, but just to be sure...do you two already know each other?"

"We dated in New York."

"I see." She raises an eyebrow. "How'd you rig this?"

"Hard work," I answer.

"Why?"

"Because she's a pain in the ass, but she's mine. Or...I want her to be. Mine."

"Okay." Her lips twitch like she wants to smile but won't give herself the pleasure...yet. "I'm Lucy Salinger. Her aunt."

"I figured."

"Between you and me?" She places a hand on my shoulder and releases a weary sigh, that small smile-to-be gaining ground. "I'm so very, *very* glad it's you, Charles Joshua Dalton."

Then she turns around, leaves the room, and closes the door behind her.

Alone for the first time since our epic kiss on the sidewalk of New York, I look down at the woman curled up on my lap and feel my heart swell with something altogether deeper than affection, something I honestly don't believe I've ever felt before.

Courtney. My Courtney. My fiancée.

"I crossed an ocean for you," I murmur, leaning down to press my lips to her forehead. And then, because the words from my favorite e.e. cummings poem suddenly spring to mind, I add, "You are the light by which my spirit is born. You are the sun, the moon, and all my stars."

"Sun…and moon," she murmurs, her chest heaving as she breathes deeply, no doubt making up for before when she couldn't catch her breath.

"You're okay," I say. "You're safe, baby."

"I thought…I thought I saw…" she whispers, "Josh."

"You did," I tell her. "It's me. I'm here."

"How?" Her eyes flutter open, and she looks up at me in a daze. "How are you here? How are you…C?"

"*Charles* Joshua Dalton," I say.

"*Charles*," she murmurs.

She looks like an angel. She looks like a woman I'd rather marry than loose. She looks like someone I'd chase halfway around the world because I couldn't imagine my life without her.

I nod, caressing her cheek with the back of my hand. "I *missed* you."

For a second, she smiles, but it disappears as she scrunches up her face, frowning at me. "I don't understand. I asked if you could offer me forever, and you said no."

"I guess I was wrong."

Her blue eyes shine as she grins at me. "You were…?"

"Wrong," I say, leaning down to press my lips briefly, fleetingly, to hers.

Her eyes reopen slowly after our kiss. "So, I'm not

crazy? Or unreasonable? Or stubborn?"

I chuckle at her. "Nope. You're still all of those things."

"So, what are you doing here?" she demands, trying to sit up.

I push gently against her lower back to give her a hand. "Marrying you, apparently."

"I was expertly arranged," she informs me.

"That's right."

"*Not* to you." She sits up straight on my lap and crosses her arms over her chest.

"Really? Because I'm CJD-underscore-NY, and I'm here, Court. I'm him. I'm the guy."

The luckiest guy in the world.

"How'd you arrange that, exactly?"

"I told the so-called experts exactly what I wanted, and they matched me with you."

Her eyes scan my face. "Really?"

"Really."

"When?"

"After we kissed."

"You went home that night and filled out an application?" She snorts. "After telling me that you *weren't* interested?"

"We went from a first kiss to you proposing in sixty seconds!" I say. "You put me on the spot, Court. I needed some time to get my head around it. I mean, give a guy a minute to consider how he wants to spend the rest of his life, huh?"

"So when exactly did you decide you wanted to do

this?"

"The *following* weekend."

She stares at me hard, then braces her hand on the back of the chair and stands up. Taking a moment to smooth out her skirt, her face is hurt and angry when she finally looks up at me.

"I had a plan—"

"I know."

"—and you *weren't* a part of it, Josh."

"Guess again," I say calmly, but inside, my stomach is in knots. She's not going to try to back out of this now, is she? Not after all of this? Not after she promised to marry me? I stand up slowly, looking down at her from my full height. "You filled out an application and I filled out an application. I never mentioned your name; I just said what I wanted. And *they* matched us. *Your* experts."

"Is this a...*joke* to you?" she asks, her voice catching on the word *joke*.

"Sure," I say, shoving my hands in my pockets. "I gave up my apartment, might lose my job, and used my pathetic savings to sign up for your stupid service, fly over here, and live in a hostel for two weeks while waiting to get married at your whim." Out of nowhere, I laugh, but it's a dry and bitter sound. "Yeah, you're right. That's pretty funny."

Her face has softened as I speak, and instead of being shaded with hurt, it's glowing with wonder as she stares at me.

"You gave up everything for me."

I don't answer. I just hold her gaze so she can see the

truth there herself.

"Why?" she asks.

Her eyes are so solemn, so steady, I feel something inside of my heart give way. I exhale a shaky breath and tell her the truth.

"Well…because I like you, Courtney Jane Salinger. I more-than-like you. I more-than-like you enough to…" I want to reach for her, but I sense we need to say these words to each other first. "I wasn't ready to let you go. I couldn't let that happen."

"But…marriage?"

"It was good enough for my parents," I say. "And yours, for that matter. Maybe we'll make it too."

"You said you weren't ready."

"Is anyone, ever?" I ask her. "Are *you*?"

"I don't know," she says, reaching up to swipe away a runaway tear. "I hope so."

"Me too." As she lowers her hand, I steal it, pressing it to my lips to swallow her tears. "Let's find out together."

A smile starts at the corners of her mouth, then slides higher and higher, growing in radiance and beauty until it takes over her entire beloved face.

"Are you sure?" she whispers.

No, but…

Still holding her hand, I lean forward and press my lips to hers. "I am."

***

An hour later, we're back at the Gretna Hall Hotel having dinner with Lucy and Melissa, but we're not Courtney

Salinger and Josh Dalton anymore.

We're Courtney and Josh Dalton.

As unbelievable as it seems, we're married.

Married.

The very concept I found so appalling the first time Courtney mentioned it at Tidewaters so many weeks ago.

Or *did* I?

There may be a fair bit of revisionist history going on in my head, but I have started to question whether Courtney's idea was somehow—deep in the recesses of my heart—more *appealing* than I want to admit. I mean, there's no question that my attraction to her, which was always quietly extant, ramped up exponentially from the moment she shared her crazy idea with me. The single-minded purity of her commitment to something so outlandish made me want to join her for the journey, made me want to be the man who went home with the prize, made me change the course of my entire life…just to be with her.

Speaking of *being with her*, I'm eager to get through this dinner and have my wife all to myself.

I squeeze her hand under the table as her Aunt Lucy raises her glass to toast us.

"Almost forty years ago," she begins, "I came to this very hotel for a wedding supper with my husband, Roland. We'd met each other at Oxford three months before and realized that our strong feelings for one another prohibited the mere concept of separation. On the night we married, I was supposed to be boarding a plane for New York. I spent that night here, in the Wakefield Suite, instead. We had no children, but we did have twenty very happy years together. He was, and he remains, the one true love of my life." She sniffles delicately before continuing, "At the time, it didn't matter that he was considerably older than I or that he was a viscount and I a commoner—and an American, to boot. It didn't matter that he was a professor and I a student. It didn't matter that neither of our families approved the match, and it didn't matter that he didn't want more children. None of it mattered because we loved each other. We *needed* to be together. We *couldn't* be apart." She pauses for a moment, tilting her head to the side. "I watched my niece's face today as she spoke her vows, and I truly believe that my Courtney Jane and her Charles Joshua have that sort of connection to one another. The kind that won't let you let go. At any rate, darlings, that's my hope for you, because you're going to need it." She lifts her champagne flute, smiling at her niece with a face shining with love. "May you love as I loved. With your whole hearts and minds, bodies and souls. May you never know a moment without its comfort or an instant away from its grasp. May it warm you on the coldest nights and light your path on the darkest days. And may that love outlast the shift of your feet upon this earth and follow you both into forever." Through tears she adds, "To the happy couple."

Melissa stands up beside her, raising her glass in one hand and squeezing Lucy around the shoulders with her other. "To the happy couple."

Beside me, Courtney sobs softly, springing up to round the table and hug her aunt. Because they're all standing up, I stand too, smiling at Aunt Lucy, who watches me over Courtney's shoulder.

"Thank you," I say, lifting my own glass to toast *her*.

Love her, she mouths, patting Courtney's back before letting her go.

Love her.

It's a simple enough request, and as Sammy pointed out, giving up my entire life in New York to follow Courtney to London speaks volumes as to my feelings, but I'm not ready to say that I love her yet. To *fall* in love with her? Yes. I smile back at Lucy, hoping that good intentions are enough for now.

"Josh," says Melissa, looking up from her phone, "all of your things have been moved from your room to Courtney's suite." She smiles at us. "This has been such a lovely celebration. But now, if you'll forgive me, I must get back to London."

"Of course," says Courtney. "Thank you for all you've done."

"Thank you for being such an easy client." Melissa looks back and forth between us, then settles on Courtney. "Your travel documents are waiting in your room. Tomorrow morning, a car will take you to the airport in Carlisle, where a helicopter will be waiting to fly you up to Inverness. From there, it's a short ride to your lodgings."

I step around the table to shake Melissa's hand. "You've been terrific."

"It was my pleasure." She nods briskly at us before leaning down to pick up her purse. "Best of luck." And then she's off.

We three are left behind to watch her go, and for a moment I wonder how long Courtney and I need to stay before we can be alone. Luckily, Aunt Lucy, about whom I'm fonder by the second, turns to us with a coy grin.

"I'm so tired," she says, faking a yawn. "Would you two mind terribly if I retired? I think I'll take off these shoes and get my old body into bed."

Yep. I'm a *big* fan of Aunt Lucy's.

"Are you sure, Aunt Lucy?" asks Courtney, taking her aunt's hands in hers. "We could stay for one more drink if you like."

"No, darling," she says, leaning forward to kiss her niece's cheek. "I'll say good-night now." She lets go of Courtney and turns to me. "Give your Aunt Lucy a kiss."

I lean down and kiss her soft cheek. "Thank you for being here."

"Thank *you* for being here," she responds with a bit of sass. "I'll say good-bye in the morning before you go."

When Lucy is out of view, Courtney turns to face me. "Well."

"Well."

She glances down at the table, then back up at me. "Is there anything else you want?"

Um. Yeah. There's *definitely* something I want.

"You mean to eat?"

"Or—or to, um, to drink?" she asks, clearing her throat.

Her eyes dart around the restaurant, landing on the bar

behind me for a second before sliding back to my face.

"No, Court," I say, stepping closer to her. "I don't want a drink."

Her tongue darts out to lick her lips. "Okay. Um, well, we could…"

I lean forward so that my lips graze her ear when I speak. "All I want…is to be alone…with my wife."

She exhales shakily against my cheek, then takes another breath that makes the tips of her breasts, covered in satin and lace, brush against my chest. I can feel them, beaded and firm, and it makes my nostrils flare with want. As *my* breath catches, she gulps softly.

"I want that too," she whispers, her lips against my skin making me want those same lips pressed against every other part of my body.

Reduced to a caveman about to have his way with the woman of his dreams, I take her hand and pull her out of the restaurant, every cell in my body aching for her, my blood coursing in hot, heavy streams to my cock, which throbs with its own heartbeat, hungry to have her.

We pause at the lift, with Courtney facing me, our chests touching with every breath. When the doors open, we step inside, our breathing synchronized in to short, shallow bursts of longing as we travel one floor higher to her suite.

In the hallway outside of our room, I don't ask for her permission—I sweep her up into my arms so that I cross the threshold holding her.

My *bride*.

My *wife*.

My *woman*.

CHAPTER 15

<u>Courtney</u>

As the door closes behind us, Josh continues through the living room into the bedroom, where he gently lowers me to the ground. My feet hit the carpet, but his arms are still around me, his chest pushing into mine with every breath he takes, his eyes dark and focused on mine.

There is this enormous part of me that feels like we should talk. There is so much to ask and to tell, so much to say, so much to find out. But another part of me says that there's no rush. After all, the miracle of us, of *now*, is that we have time.

"What are you thinking?" he asks, his voice low and gruff.

"That we have plenty of time," I answer.

His shoulders slump just a touch.

"Oh!" I say. "But that doesn't mean I *need* time. I mean, I *don't* need time. Or *more* time. I mean, I'm ready. Not that *I* have to—or *we* have to—I mean, I'm—"

"Nervous."

A short burst of laughter slips from my lips. "Yes."

"Why?"

"Because…" I feel breathless and I have no idea why I'm whispering. "I want…um…"

"Me?" he asks. "Do you want me?"

I nod. "I do."

"I'm yours," he answers, leaning forward to press his forehead to mine.

"We belong to each other," I say, marveling in the words even as I say them.

He leans away from me and his eyes widen for a second before he blinks, then forces a weak smile.

"What are *you* thinking?" I ask him.

"It's wild, isn't it? What we just did?"

I step out of his arms because if I don't take these shoes off, I think I might lose feeling in my feet. I sit down in a puffy floral chair in the corner of the room.

"Yes," I say, looking up at him. "It could have been anyone, but it was you."

I lean forward to remove my shoes, wincing with pain, and suddenly Josh is kneeling before me.

"Your feet hurt?" he asks me, his eyebrows furrowing, his lips turning down.

"Mm-hm. My shoes are too tight."

He picks up my right foot and takes off the shoe, then does the same with my left. I lean back in the chair and sigh with relief as his hands cup my foot and start to gently massage it. He doesn't look up at me but concentrates on his work, his thumbs working in a circular motion to ease the tension in my muscles.

"Oh, my God," I half-sigh, half-moan, "that feels so

good."

The bedroom is dimly lit, with the only light coming through the door from the sitting room, but it catches the copper highlights in his dark-brown hair.

"When you were little," I ask, "were you a redhead?"

He looks up at me and grins. "Yeah. How'd you know?"

"Your hair has flecks of red in it."

"So does yours," he says, switching feet and eliciting another low moan from me. "Jesus, Court."

"What?"

"You're moaning."

"It feels *amazing*."

He pauses for a second, then takes a deep breath and lets it go slowly as he continues massaging. "Do you know what it does to a man? To make a woman moan like that?"

I grin at him. "Do you know what it does to a woman? To rub her feet like this?"

"My wife likes having her feet rubbed," he says softly, as though making a mental note.

But it's his use of the word *wife* that makes my heart swell to bursting. This beautiful man kneeling at my feet is my husband. My *husband*. I gulp with the magnitude of it, the goodness of it.

Reaching forward, I run my fingers through his hair, watching as the dark tendrils thread through my pale fingers.

"Thank you for my ring," I say. "That was a surprise."

He looks up at me and grins. "When I got your text last night, I thought about how it would've felt to get that text back in New York. How *terrible* it would have felt. When I got off the train, I stopped by a little shop in town and bought it for you."

"Off the…?"

"Train."

"You lost your passport!" I say.

"Yeah!" he says, his face bemused. "How'd you…oh, my God! Were you on the same train?"

Laughing, I nod at him. "I heard your name. 'Passenger Dalton.' I suddenly missed you so much, I didn't know what to do with myself."

"So you texted me that you were getting married."

"Yes." I reach for his cheeks and cradle his face between my palms. His hands have stopped moving on my feet as he gazes up at me. "I couldn't stop thinking about you. Thank you for coming. Thank you for being here."

His eyes search mine for a long moment before he slides his hands up my arms to hold my wrists. "I care about you."

"I know."

"I should have told you. I should have said it. That night, I made *you* say it, but I didn't—"

"Shhh," I hush him, nuzzling his nose with mine, his warm breath fanning my face. "You're here."

"I'm here," he says, touching his lips to mine.

He lets go of my wrists and cups my face, kissing me tenderly, his lips soft but insistent as he rises to his knees to get closer. His tongue touches mine, and I slide forward to the edge of the chair to get closer to him. We don't stop kissing as I slip my hands into his suit jacket and smooth it over his shoulders. His hands slide down my neck to the zipper of my gown.

He stands up and looks down at me with a slight smile on his slick lips, holding out his hand. I take it, letting him pull me up. Standing on tiptoes, I flatten my hands on his chest and kiss him as he draws the zipper the rest of the way down my back.

My fingers land on the buttons of his white shirt as his tongue sweeps into my mouth again. I meet it with mine, sighing as my fingers work quickly to open his shirt, my knuckles skimming the warm expanse of his chest with each button I open.

He pushes my dress over my shoulders, and it falls around my feet in a swoosh of fabric. Standing in my white bra and matching panties, my nipples harden into stiff points, straining for release, as my fingers land on the button of his pants. I unsnap it and tug at the zipper before backing up to the bed and lying down.

A moment later, the warm weight of his body covers mine as he kisses a trail from the base of my throat to my lips, then rests there, stealing my breath and sharing his. We kiss until our lips ache and his erection, stiff as stone, pushes against me through the thin barrier of our underwear.

He rolls me slightly toward him to unlatch my strapless bra, and I run my fingers down his back to the waistband of his boxers, pushing them over his hips. He stands up to get rid of them, then reaches for my panties and slides them down my legs so we're both naked.

Kneeling between my legs with his hands braced on either side of my waist, he looks down at me with almost-black eyes outlined with thin bands of cerulean.

"We're moving fast," he says, a slight pant making his words breathless. "Are you okay?"

I reach for his neck and draw his face closer to mine. "I'm fine."

His lips claim mine in a passionate kiss before skimming down the column of my throat to my chest. Sucking one of my nipples into his mouth, he laves it with his tongue, licking and tasting until I moan loudly, writhing beneath him. My hands plunge into his hair as he moves to the other side, licking a slow circle around the nipple before teasing it with his lips and tongue.

Arching back against the mattress, I bury my head in the pillow and close my eyes as his lips scorch a trail from my breasts to the throbbing spot at the apex of my thighs. His nose separates my nether lips and his tongue follows, stroking hot and wet over my aching clit, which makes me cry out. I throw an arm over my head, and my fingers dig into the sheets as he continues to love the pulsing nub of my flesh, sucking it between his lips before gentling the sharp sensation with a long stroke of his tongue. I can barely catch my breath and my hips have risen off the bed when an orgasm tears through me, making stars explode behind my eyelids and tears slide from the corners of my eyes.

He shifts back up and over me, bracing his elbows on either side of my head. I am panting and breathless when I finally open my eyes and look into his.

"Fuck, that was beautiful," he whispers, licking my lips before kissing them.

I can taste myself on his tongue, which makes the tremors in clit intensify for an extra moment of aftershocks. I am soaked and ready for him when I whisper, "I need you, Josh. Please."

"Are you on the pill?" he asks.

I swallow and nod, though somewhere, in the back of my mind, it occurs to me that this isn't like having sex with some guy I've dated a few times. This is Josh. This is my husband.

"You *married* me," I say, reaching up to cup his beautiful face. "Why did you do that?"

"I was matched to you," he answers, his lips tilting up a touch as his lips brush against mine.

"I don't want you to regret it."

"I made my own choice, baby. You let me go, remember?" He reaches up to caress my cheek and gives me a look. "You told me to have the best life ever."

Remembering that night is sweet and bitter at the same time. It stings, but it's also a part of Josh's and my complicated history, an intrinsic part of us.

"Well," he says, moving his body over mine, his erection sliding easily between the slick, hot folds of still-pulsating flesh between my thighs, "that's exactly what I'm doing."

A sound of pure need escapes from the back of my throat, half-moan and half-whimper, as my hips rise to meet his.

"Please," I murmur, burying my head in the pillow.

"Please what?" he teases, lining up the tip of his sex at the opening of mine.

"I want you inside me," I say, the lips of my sex contracting, try to pull him in.

"My wife," he says softly.

"Forever," I gasp as he slides forward, filling me completely.

My hands slide to his buttocks, holding them tightly, forcing him to stay buried deep inside of me. He's thick and throbbing, stretching me, owning me, buried inside of me. Now that he's mine, I never, ever want to let him go.

"*Fuck*," he whispers, resting his sweaty forehead on mine. "Court, you're...*perfect.*"

The walls of my cunt squeeze him so tightly that I can feel two heartbeats—his and mine.

"More," I sigh, digging my nails into his skin and drawing them from his ass to his back.

He gasps, withdrawing almost completely before surging into me again.

"More."

"*Courtney, Courtney, Courtney,*" he murmurs near my ear before skimming his lips back to mine.

As he kisses me, his hips begin to move in a steady motion, faster and faster, pistoning in and out of my body, our panting breath swallowed by each other as he growls into my mouth and his tongue tangles with mine. He grabs my hands and laces our fingers together over my head as his movements quicken. The friction of his hot, rigid flesh dragging against my trembling walls makes another orgasm gather inside of me until I can't hold it back. It explodes like a bomb within me, with rings of tremors fanning out in short, fast bursts to clasp him in undulating waves, wringing his own pleasure from mine. He throws back his head, calls out my name, and erupts, convulsing in rapid quakes and coming in hot, thick streams inside of me.

Time becomes relative as we hold each other close, as our breathing slowly returns to normal. At some point, he withdraws from me and pulls me tenderly against him, my back to his chest. My body is sated, and my eyes are so heavy, I can't open them.

Josh adjusts his arm around me, flattening his hand under my breasts as he exhales warm breath against the back of my neck. There is so much to say, so much to talk about, but all of it can wait.

We are married.

Nestled in the sanctuary of my husband's arms, I sleep.

***

During the night, Josh reaches for me again, primally and half-asleep. His fingers stroke my nipples into hard points and his erection pushes against my naked bottom. I scissor my legs, spreading them for him, and he enters me easily, my cunt still hot and wet from before.

Our lovemaking is calmer this time, more tender, less hurried. He pulls my face to his and kisses me tenderly over my shoulder as he slides in and out of my body, his palm flat over my breast, which he grasps and squeezes as he comes inside of me.

I don't orgasm this time, but I don't need to. I'm still sated from before, and he gathers me back into his arms, still buried deep within me, as we fall back to sleep.

When I wake up in the morning, I am alone, with the comforter pulled up to my shoulders. I can hear the shower running, and though I have half a thought to join him, half of me is shy too, despite everything we did last night. I don't know if he likes showering with someone. That's something I'll need to find out.

Instead, I dial zero for room service and order coffee, tea, juice, and a basket of baked goods.

"How do you take your coffee?" asks the receptionist.

"With cream and sugar."

"No need for milk then?"

Hmm. Does Josh drink coffee? If so, what does he like in it?

Because I have no idea, I also order milk, cream, sugar, sweetener, and honey.

She tells me our breakfast will be up in about an hour.

When I hang up the phone, I consider for a moment that I am married to someone about whom I know so little. I have no idea if he likes company in the shower or if he drinks coffee, and if he does, what he likes in it. We're not strangers, of course. Technically, I've known Josh for over a year. But the Josh who makes me gimlets and was my friend in New York City is different from the Josh who's showering in the next room. And frankly, there's a shit-ton I don't know about my husband. There are massive gaps in my knowledge of him, and that learning curve feels a little overwhelming.

"Good morning."

I look up as Josh opens the bathroom door and steps into our room wearing a towel around his waist and another hanging from his neck. His hair is glistening with beads of water and his chest is slick. Last night, it was too dark to see much of him, but this morning, I can gawk—er, um, *admire him*—all I want.

His body is lean but chiseled, like he takes good care of it, and suddenly I flash back to the times he jumped over the bar at Tidewaters. Women were always flirting with him there, and I wonder, fleetingly, how many have had the opportunity to see him like this.

I lean up on one elbow. "Good morning."

He scrubs at his ears with the towel. "How do you feel?"

"Awesome," I say. "I ordered coffee and breakfast. Do you *drink* coffee?"

"Yeah. Sometimes."

"How can you drink coffee *sometimes*?"

He shrugs. "I don't always feel like it."

"It doesn't work like that. You have it every morning or never."

"No. *You* have it every morning or never. I have it sometimes."

"Hmm."

"Hmm."

He grins at me, throwing the towel around his neck on the floor as he approaches the bed, but I miss his rippling abs on full display, because I'm staring at the damp towel lying in a heap on the rug.

When he gets to the bed, he squats down, leveling his eyes with mine.

"Hi."

"Hi."

"Stop looking at the towel I just threw on the floor. The maids will get it."

That makes me smile, and my smile turns into a giggle when he climbs on top of me and kisses me. The comforter separates his clean body from my dirty one, and I can't deny it: even after having sex twice last night, I feel deprived. I want more.

But even more than sex? I want a shower.

"I'm filthy," I say.

"Fuck yes, you are."

He kisses me again, and I wind my arms around his neck. "You're clean and you smell nice."

"My wife likes a clean-smelling man."

"Hey." I narrow my eyes at him. "You did that last night too."

"What?"

"You were taking notes about me liking my feet rubbed."

"I'm keeping track." He nuzzles my nose with his. "I want to make you happy. I promised, remember?"

"No. When? In New York?"

His eyes widen. "No. In my e-mail. I said I'd do everything I can to make you happy."

Ohhhh. Yeah. Of course.

"I think there's a disconnect in my head between you and C," I say.

"I *am* C."

"I know. But for two weeks, C was just…C. An unknown. A stranger." His eyes are so blue, staring into mine, they make my heart race with attraction and affection—and something altogether deeper and more complicated than either of those feelings. "What did you mean in your e-mail when you said that maybe we had different reasons for doing this?"

"You did it to get married to *someone*." He takes a deep breath and sighs. "I did it to marry *you*."

"How'd you know you'd get me? They could've matched you with anyone."

He shakes his head. "Because I described *you* as perfectly as I could."

"You loaded your answers to raise your odds."

"That makes it sound like a cheated, but I didn't." His jaw tightens. "I was honest."

I look away from him, feeling unsettled.

"Hey. What's going on in your head?" he asks.

"If I'd been arranged with someone totally anonymous, I'd know that he approached Arrange Me Too with the same intentions as me, with the same level of expectation," I say. "I guess…I just hope that you never blame me for this."

"*Blame* you?"

"Yeah. Like, maybe you thought you were saving me or something. But I didn't *ask* to be saved. I didn't *want* to be saved."

He huffs softly as he rolls onto his back beside me. We're quiet for a moment, and it's a tense silence I wish he would break by saying something sweet and reassuring that will make it all better, but he doesn't. When he does speak, his voice is low and dull, like he's annoyed with me.

"I already told you that you didn't force me. I wanted to be with you, Courtney. I was clear about that."

"But you didn't want to *marry* me."

"I changed my mind," he snaps. "Is that okay with you?"

His tone surprises me and clues me into the fact that I'm pushing him a little too much too quick. Whatever his reasons were, the deed is done. We're married. Maybe I shouldn't keep rehashing his reasons why, but I can't help feeling like whatever they are, they're going to bite me in the ass later.

"Yeah," I say softly. "It's okay. I'm happy it was you."

"Then let that be enough for now," he says, his voice gentler than before as he props himself up on an elbow to look at me. "Hey, where are we going today? Did I hear something about a helicopter ride?"

"Mm-hm," I say, grinning at him. "We're going north to Inverness. I have no idea where we're staying or what we're doing once we get there, but…"

In one smooth move, he lifts the comforter and joins me under the covers. He reaches for me, pulling me into his arms. "More of this. That's what we're doing."

As he nuzzles my neck with his clean-shaven face, I sigh, because he's warm and smooth and smells like heaven.

"I'm filthy, remember?"

His hand slides down my stomach and into the valley of trimmed curls that hide my clit. He circles the pulsing bud with his finger while I reach for him and untuck the towel around his waist. I arch my back against the bed and moan softly as he inserts two fingers inside of me, still massaging my clit with gentle, insistent thumb strokes.

"Then we'll have to take a shower together," he suggests, kissing my throat.

When I giggle, he probably has no idea why, but it's only because a question I had about my husband has just been answered: he *does* like taking showers together.

Surely, this is how it will be, I think. Learning a little bit more about each other day by glorious day.

I whimper as he skims his lips down my chest and his mouth takes over for his fingers.

No more laughing.

Just bliss.

***

Because today is clear and sunny, the helicopter ride is amazing.

Seated side by side, holding hands and wearing headphones, we have a narrated tour of Scotland from Gretna Green, over the moors and hills of Ettrick to Falkirk, up north of Pitlochry, and above the craggy lands of Cairngorms all the way to the wee airport at Inverness, where we land on the private side of the airfield, near the Highland Aviation flight school.

After thanking our pilot, we are led to a private car that

takes us to the Beach Cottage B&B on the shores of the Moray Firth. Melissa has booked the entire two-suite cottage for us, and after a warm welcome from the innkeeper and her husband, we're handed the keys to our own private cottage. Though we have both bedrooms at our disposal, we choose to stay in the Moray Room with its Juliet balcony that overlooks the beach and firth beyond. I swing open the French doors and grasp the waist-high railing, breathing in the fresh air.

Josh comes up behind me, caging me between him and the balcony as his hands land on the railing just outside of mine. He rests his chin on my shoulder.

"This is amazing."

"I agree. Melissa should be sainted."

"I love that we have the whole place to ourselves," he says, lifting my hair to kiss the side of my neck.

"Better than a shoebox in Hell's Kitchen?" I ask.

"Anywhere with you is better," he says. "But yeah. This is pretty spectacular, Mrs. Dalton."

I gasp softly. "Mrs. Dalton!"

"I just wanted to try it out." He chuckles against my neck. "You don't have to change your name for me."

"I *want* to." I turn in his arms to face him, reaching for his face with a smile that must be beaming. "Of course I will. Courtney Dalton. Courtney Salinger Dalton."

"It sounds very literary," he says, kissing my nose.

"Perfect for the wife of a playwright."

"*My wife*," he says softly. "How long will it take for me to get used to that, I wonder?"

"Take your time," I tell him, turning back around to look at the view but leaning against my husband. "Speaking of Daltons…did you tell them yet? Your parents? Your brothers?"

He takes a deep breath and sighs, and I'm starting to learn that this is a tell of his. It belies a heaviness. "No. You?"

"No," I say softly. "Aunt Lucy wanted me to call my dad, but…"

"You didn't know what to say."

"I didn't," I say. "I also didn't want them to stop me."

His chin is back on my shoulder. "Mine are going to be hurt."

"Mine too," I say, swallowing over a sudden and unexpected lump in my throat. "How about we figure it out once we get home? Don't let's spoil these few days?"

"Agreed," he says, moving his hands from the railing to clasp them around me instead. "Speaking of home…I don't have one anymore."

I turn in his arms. "Move in with me."

"You wouldn't mind?"

"Mind? You're my husband. Where else would you live? With your ex-girlfriend?"

"Sammy and I broke up a million years ago. She's not a threat to you."

"Good," I say, but I still don't want my husband anywhere near her.

He's quiet for a long moment, and when I look up, his eyes are fixed on something far away, over my shoulder.

"Are you thinking about her?"

"No. I'm just thinking...I mean..." He shakes his head, and his eyes are troubled when he glances at me for a second. "I don't have much to offer you."

"What do you mean?"

"I couldn't even afford to come here without giving up my apartment. I have very little savings. Crappy insurance. I bartend to subsidize my writing."

"Hey, look at me," I say, reaching for his chin and forcing him to meet my eyes. "I didn't ask for a millionaire. My salary and benefits are really good. We'll be fine."

He winces, then drops my gaze. "My father was a good provider. He took pride in it."

"That's great, but that was your parents' marriage. Ours will be different. Whatever we make it. Whatever we want it to be. Maybe I'll support you for a while, until one of your plays is a hit. And then you can support me later when—"

I stop myself just in time, glad he's not looking at me, except he chooses that moment to look up.

"What?" he asks, with a teasing smile. "When...what?"

"Nothing," I say, feeling my cheeks flush red.

"Come on. Tell me. What do you want? You want to go back to school?"

"No." I clear my throat. "I was going to say, maybe if we have *kids* someday, you can support me while I stay home with—"

"Kids!" he exclaims, his arms falling from around me to his sides. His eyes are wide and wild as he stares at me. "Jesus, Courtney!"

"I'm not saying I want them tomorrow!" I insist. "Or, I don't know. I mean, I want kids someday. Don't you want kids?"

"I…I don't know," he says, staring at me wide-eyed and dragging his hands through his hair. "I—I haven't thought a lot about them. I mean, someday. Maybe. Yeah. But not for a long time. I don't—I don't—"

"I'm sorry," I say, reaching for him. "We don't have to talk about this—"

"We just got married," he says, taking a step away from me. "Like, not even twenty-four hours ago. Could we just get used to *that* for a little while?"

Tears spring into my eyes, and I blink them away because I can see that I've completely freaked him out, and that was never my intention. I feel ridiculous and needy, pushy and absurd.

"I'm sorry," I tell him. "I was just…daydreaming."

"Could you possibly *not* daydream about kids yet?"

Feeling miserable, I nod, turning away from the now spoiled view. I don't know where to look or what to do, but when my eyes settle on my suitcase, I cross the room to snap it open and unpack. As I reach up to wipe away a rogue tear, his hands land on my shoulders. I spin in an instant, resting my cheek against his chest.

"I'm s-sorry," I say with a pathetic sniffle.

His arms come around me, and I feel a wave of relief as he holds me close.

"Courtney, Courtney, Courtney," he says softly, almost singing my name like a lullaby. "You don't have to move so

231

fast."

"I don't know how else to move."

"I need you to slow down so I can catch up."

"I don't want kids yet."

"At least we agree on that," he says, rubbing my back and pressing a kiss on the top of my head.

"Are you mad at me?" I ask, the sound muffled against his shirt.

"No," he says. "Not mad. Just…slow down a little, okay? We've got a long way to go, Court. We're just starting."

"I'll try. I promise."

I look up at him and nod, and he smiles down at me, wiping away my tears with his thumbs. "How about a walk on the beach, Mrs. Dalton? We've got plenty of time before lunch."

"Yeah. I'd like that. Give me a minute?"

I slip into the bathroom and splash my face with cold water, determined to concentrate on being a newlywed and living in the moment with Josh instead of focusing on a future with too many unanswered questions to count.

CHAPTER 16

Josh

Four days later, our Highlands honeymoon is almost over.

Once thing about my marriage is absolutely certain: our chemistry is combustible, and we can't seem to get enough of each other.

We have sex everywhere; in both beds, in both sitting rooms, with Courtney braced against the balcony, on the sofas, in the shower, and even skinny-dipping one warm evening in the firth. We fall asleep naked in each other's arms, limbs entangled, and wake up at least once during the night to fuck again before morning. She's a vocal lover, moaning and whimpering, crying out when her orgasm hits and sighing as she falls asleep. I catalog her noises, listening for them each in turn, and feeling an insane amount of pleasure that I'm able to unravel this woman so completely, that I can make her body shatter with mine. Knowing that I can satisfy Courtney sexually makes me feel that I can at least offer her *something*.

That said, every time I turn my mind to her supporting me financially, I picture my father's face, and it makes me feel nauseous. He won't understand, and I'm afraid I'll lose his respect, which is no small thing. I don't live near my parents, but I love them and have always sought their approval. Marrying Courtney so impulsively is already going to hurt and upset them; appearing like I'm sponging off of my wife will just add disgust to their disappointment.

As Courtney and I walked on the beach last Sunday afternoon, as a means toward living in the moment and not stressing about the future, we agreed to turn off our phones until we were headed home. It's been an amazing four days of walks and swims, laughing under the sheets, and swapping childhood tales over Scottish dinners. A perfect fantasy honeymoon.

God, I'm not ready to leave.

Maybe that's why I'm up so early, standing naked by the window, watching the early morning sun rise over the firth. I wish we could hide away here in Scotland for a few more weeks, making love every night and falling harder for each other every day. I wish we could ignore the fact that our flight from Inverness to New York leaves at 1:25pm this afternoon.

But we can't.

Today is Thursday, and real life is bearing down on us like a fast-moving storm. At some point, we're going to have to turn our phones back on and face the fact that we have no idea how to build a life together.

I turn away from the sparkling water to look at my wife, and I can't help the possessiveness that clutches my heart, the intense tenderness that draws every cell in my body to a corresponding cell in hers.

Yeah, today is scary.

Tomorrow will be scary too.

But I wouldn't trade the gold band on my finger for a do-over.

She's mine, and I'm hers. Marriages built on less have survived. I have to believe ours will too.

"Hmmm. Mmmm."

Did I mention that Courtney sometimes hums herself awake?

She does.

And I fucking love it.

Her honey-blonde hair is fanned out over the white pillow, and the quilt on the bed has slipped just enough to reveal one rosebud nipple. It's standing proud and pretty against her white skin, like it knows I'm watching, and I feel blood rush, hot and fast, to my cock. My balls tighten as my erection swells. I skim my fingers over my chest and reach for the stiffening flesh, stroking it lightly as I cross the room and climb onto the bed.

My body depresses the mattress, and her eyes slowly open. As she focuses on my face, her lips tilt up in a smile.

"You're…up," she says, chuckling as her glance flicks to my erection.

"Last day," I say, lying down on my side.

"Shhh," she says, rolling onto her side to face me. "Don't say it or it might come true."

"No way around it, baby."

I dip my head and kiss her nipple, because it's daring me to.

"Mmmm," she moans. "Will you still do this in New York?"

"No," I say, letting my breath feather softly over her sensitive skin. "I only have sex with my wife in Scotland."

"Then let's move to Scotland," she says, pulling down the quilt, then kicking it off. She slides a touch closer to me so that the tips of her breasts brush my chest.

I wish.

"What time is the car coming?"

"Eleven thirty," she says.

"What do you want to until then?"

She flattens her hands on my chest and pushes me onto my back. As she kisses her way from my chest to my abdomen, I tangle my fingers in her hair, my ass and balls tightening with sweet anticipation. I groan her name as she takes the rigid length of my erection between her lips and bathes me in her mouth.

I don't want to think about where Courtney learned to do the things she knows how to do, but fuck, my woman knows how to give head. As wet as a warm bath, she winds her tongue around my cock, occasionally looking up at me with her innocent blue eyes. Her lips inch down, little by little, until she deep throats me, and it feels so fucking unbelievable, I clench my eyes shut and throw an arm over my head.

"Fuuuuuck, Court."

"Mmmm," she hums, working my shaft with her tongue while I pump in and out of her mouth.

I lean up and look over her head to see my balls pressed

against her cheek, and that's when I come because the image of my beautiful, naked wife balls-deep with my cock in her mouth is pretty much the hottest thing I've ever seen.

I'm hard as stone even after she swallows, so she straddles my lap, guiding my slick cock into her slippery pussy. With her hands braced on my chest and my hands gripping her hips, she sets the pace and rhythm of our fucking, rocking back and forth, her perfect tits on full display and those stunning eyes locked on mine.

It should be *too* intense to watch another human being as fiercely as we watch each other, joined as intimately as we are, but I can't look away and she doesn't.

Maybe we're trying to hold on to these last exquisite moments of feeling like the only two people in the whole world. Maybe we're trying to cement this bond so that it carries over to home. Maybe we are just intensely turned on by the way we fit together and how much pleasure we can offer one another.

Or maybe—just maybe—this is the beginning of my wife and I falling in love with each other, and it would be wrong—so *fucking* wrong—to miss a single moment.

She sits up and reaches between us, sliding her middle finger over her clit, and her moans quickly turn into cries. When she's on the brink of coming, I jackknife into a sitting position and smash my mouth into hers, pumping wildly into her body as my tongue tangles mindlessly with hers.

We are breathless and panting, holding onto each other as tightly as we can, when I realize that she's crying. She rests her cheek on my shoulder and her hot tears slip down my arm.

I don't ask her why.

Part of me feels like crying too.

I just close my eyes and hold on.

***

"Did you want to grab some shortbread for Dina?"

She nods, holding my arm for balance as she slips her feet back into her shoes just outside of security.

I lean down and kiss her cheek, then lace our fingers together and steer us toward the Duty-Free store.

"Do you want to get anything for your parents?" I ask.

"Umm. No," she says.

Since we arrived at the airport, we've been in constant motion: checking in, checking our bags, and passing through security. For the first time, I realize she's a little quiet, a little withdrawn. Or maybe this is just "travel" Courtney? We've never traveled together. I have no idea.

I squeeze her hand and point out a display of cookies in festive red plaid boxes. "One for her and one for us?"

"Yeah. Sure."

I drop her hand and grab two boxes.

"Do you want anything else?" I ask. "Scotch? A bagpipe magnet? We could see if they have some haggis."

She gives me a half-smile. "No, thanks."

"Hey," I say. "Are you okay?"

"What if we stayed one more day?" she asks in a rush.

"Our bags are checked." I rest the cookies on the shelf and put my arms around her, drawing her close to me. "Only the honeymoon's ending, baby. We're just beginning."

"I know," she says, her expression wistful. "I just wish we had more time."

I lean down and kiss her. "Wasn't that the whole point? We have forever, Mrs. Dalton."

She's still giving me that timid half-smile, and I wish I knew what to do to make it go away.

Make her a gimlet and ask her about her day, says the voice in my head, which is utterly absurd and makes me a little sad, because it highlights the fact that I really don't know how to make her feel better outside of Tidewaters.

"We're going to make it, aren't we?" she whispers. "We're going to be okay?"

She's searching my eyes so gravely, it makes me desperate to comfort her.

"Yeah," I say, holding her closer. "Of course."

"Okay," she says softly. "Okay."

"Hey, I know. When we get home, let's make a date to see a show. A musical."

Finally her smile deepens, and her voice warms up a little. "Yes! A show. What a great idea. I'd love that, Josh."

Something fisting inside of me loosens a touch. *See that?* it says, patting me on the back. *You did it! You made her feel a little better.*

"You know what?" I say, letting her go and picking up the cookies to take them to the cash register. "We should turn our phones back on."

Her smile instantly disappears. "We should?"

"Court," I say, smiling at her and trying to sound confident, "we're going home, and we're going to be okay."

"You don't know that."

"We promised. I gave you my word, remember? To have and hold?" I remind her. "In sickness and in health. Until death." I search her eyes, willing her to get on board this train with me. "I'm not dead yet."

She takes a deep breath and nods. "Me neither."

I give the cashier my last British pounds for the cookies, and we step out of the store and into the terminal area.

"Okay," she says, exhaling a breath she must have been holding. "We have thirty minutes. Phones on?"

I grin at her. "That's my girl."

We find two seats by the windows, remove our backpacks, and sit down, taking out our phones and powering them on.

"It's all going to be okay," I tell her. "We're going to have a great life together, baby."

"You're right." She smiles at me bravely and nods. "It's all going to be okay."

Our phones ding, beep, and buzz, and we giggle at each other before looking down to see who's been looking for us while we were blissfully off the grid.

I have over a dozen text messages and a few voice mails too.

The first text is from Lulu, sent today, asking if I have any idea when and if I'll be back at Tidewaters because she's starting to make the July schedule.

Hmm. That's a conversation Courtney and I going to need to have sooner rather than later. I get the feeling she doesn't want me to go back to work at Tidewaters, but I feel really strongly about making my own money and contributing to our finances.

The next text is from my brother. He tells me that my parents are worried about me and asks that I please get in touch with them.

That's when I realize that I missed our usual Sunday afternoon phone call. Fuck.

The next text thread is from Sammy. I tap on the thread and see that she's sent me more than half of the dozen messages. I scroll back to read the first one, and my mouth drops open when I read: *Max and I broke up. I need you. I really need you, Josh. Please call me.*

"Everything okay?" asks Courtney.

I gulp, jerking the phone out of her view. Just this morning she referred to Sammy as my "ex." The last thing she needs to know is that Sammy's been texting me all week.

"Lulu wants to know when I'm coming back to work."

"Oh!" she says. "Are you—are you going back to Tidewaters? I thought…"

"What?"

"I mean, I can support us," she says. "You don't have to bartend, or—or work nights anymore. You can concentrate on your—"

"I need to make money too, Court."

"Why?"

"Because I do. Because I'm not a freeloader."

"Josh! I never said you were a—"

"Let's shelve it for now and talk about it when we get

home, okay?"

"Sure." She leans away from me a little. "Anything else?"

"I missed my Sunday phone call with my parents. They're worried. My brother reamed me out."

"Oh, no," she says, her face falling. "Text them back! Let them know you're okay."

"Yeah," I say, nodding at her with a weak smile. "I'm about to. How about you? Everything okay?"

"I had a bunch of X-rated texts from Dina," she says, grinning at me. "Lots and lots of suggestions for us. Mostly…positions."

"Any good ones?"

"Believe it or not, we covered most of them."

"I believe it," I say, a montage of sex with Courtney flashing through my mind. "Read the others to me."

"No way!" she says, hitting my arm lightly. Then she takes a deep breath and lets it go. "Oh. Also, my boss wants me to go to Tokyo next week."

"Japan?" I exclaim.

She nods. "Yeah. Just for two days. Well, four with the travel. Leave on Monday, back on Thursday."

"Wow. So, um, you're going to Japan next week?"

Honestly? I hate the idea. I hate the thought of being apart for four days, and I really hate the thought of her being so far away.

"I don't have to," she says quickly, reading my face. "He just suggested…"

Don't be a controlling asshole, Josh.

"If you need to go to Japan, you should go."

"They liked the job I did in London. They want me to replicate some of the practices I put in place in other international branches." She puts her hand on my knee. "Hey! Why don't you come with me?"

"To Japan?"

"Sure! I'll trade in my business-class ticket for two coach. We'll extend our honeymoon!"

"Courtney, I can't just go to Tokyo."

"Why not?"

"I need to get back to the New Dramatists before they give my seat away. I have work to do."

"Can't you—"

"No, baby, I can't. I've already been away for three weeks."

"Okay," she says, sighing softly as her smile dims. "Sorry. You know I'm proud of you, right? I can't wait to read your plays. I want to be supportive."

"I know. It's fine. Sorry I snapped at you." I tilt my head to the side. "I'm going to write back to my folks, okay?"

"Yeah. Definitely," she says, nodding at me.

I skip the rest of Sam's texts and open the text threads from my mother and father. On Sunday they're surprised, by Monday they're worried, and by today they're frantic. Shit. Shit. Shit.

Mom and Dad, I write, *I'm really sorry I worried you. I lost my charger here in London and couldn't find one that worked with my phone. I'll call you on Sunday when I'm back in New York. Sorry, again. Love, Josh xo*

Just as I press "Send," Courtney, who has her phone pressed to her ear, gasps, her body going rigid and her face turning white as she listens to a message.

"Oh, no," she whimpers, letting the phone fall to her lap. "No. No, no, no. Oh, no."

I'm instantly on high-alert. "Court? Baby, what happened? Courtney?"

I reach for her, but she springs up and sprints to the large plate-glass window in the waiting area and stands there, looking out at the tarmac. She shoves her phone in her back pocket and crosses her arms over her chest, rocking back and forth from foot to foot.

Everything in me tenses as I watch her. *Whatever this is, it's bad.* I put my own phone away and follow her. I don't touch her; I just stand beside her.

"What happened?" I finally ask.

"Aunt Lucy," she whispers. "She…she called my father. She told him. About us. About everything."

The blood drains from my face, and my heart starts racing.

"W-what? Why?"

"Does it matter?"

She inhales sharply, and I realize she's desperately fighting back tears, her face utterly shattered.

"Court," I say softly, wanting to pull her into my arms but also sensing that she needs her space, "it's going to be okay."

When she looks up at me, my heart squeezes from the

pain in her eyes.

"He's furious. He's threatening to disinherit me."

"We'll talk to him. We'll go out to Connecticut next weekend and talk to them together."

"He doesn't want to see me."

Her hands are buried tightly in her elbows, but I tug one free and lace my fingers through hers, grateful when she doesn't pull away from me.

"He's just mad. But you're his only child." I squeeze her fingers gently. "He'll forgive you."

"Shhh," she murmurs, hushing me like she can't bear anymore platitudes, anymore hollow assurances that "everything will be okay," however well meaning.

She stares forlornly out the window, and my gaze follows hers, landing on the dark clouds in the distance.

Around us, the airport buzzes with activity.

Gate announcements are made.

Flights take off and land.

People rush by us and babies cry and the world keeps on moving...

...while my bride and I stand side by side in front of the airport window, still as stone, hand in hand, our eyes on the storm approaching from the west, from New York City, where our abandoned lives are waiting to be jump-started once again.

THE END

THANK YOU FOR READING ARRANGE ME!

For the continuation of Courtney and Josh's story, look for
the sequel to this book, titled ARRANGE US, available for
preorder on Amazon now!

** AVAILABLE ON MAY 20th **

ALSO AVAILABLE
from Katy Regnery

a modern fairytale
(A collection)

The Vixen and the Vet
Never Let You Go
Ginger's Heart
Dark Sexy Knight
Don't Speak
Shear Heaven
Fragments of Ash
Swan Song (coming 2019)

THE BLUEBERRY LANE SERIES

THE ENGLISH BROTHERS
(Blueberry Lane Books #1–7)

Breaking Up With Barrett
Falling for Fitz
Anyone but Alex
Seduced by Stratton
Wild about Weston
Kiss Me Kate
Marrying Mr. English

THE WINSLOW BROTHERS
(Blueberry Lane Books #8–11)

Bidding on Brooks
Proposing to Preston
Crazy about Cameron
Campaigning for Christopher

THE ROUSSEAUS
(Blueberry Lane Books #12–14)

Jonquils for Jax
Marry Me Mad
J.C. and the Bijoux Jolis

THE STORY SISTERS
(Blueberry Lane Books #15–17)

The Bohemian and the Businessman
The Director and Don Juan
Countdown to Midnight

THE SUMMERHAVEN SERIES

Fighting Irish
Smiling Irish
Loving Irish
Catching Irish

THE ARRANGED DUO

Arrange Me
Arrange Us

STAND-ALONE BOOKS:

After We Break
(a stand-alone second-chance romance)

Frosted
(a stand-alone romance novella for mature readers)

Unloved, a love story
(a stand-alone suspenseful romance)

Under the paranormal pen name
K. P. Kelley

It's You, Book 1
It's You, Book 2

Under the YA pen name
Callie Henry

A Date for Hannah

ABOUT THE AUTHOR

New York Times and *USA Today* bestselling author **Katy Regnery** started her writing career by enrolling in a short story class in January 2012. One year later, she signed her first contract, and Katy's first novel was published in September 2013.

More than forty books later, Katy claims authorship of the multititled *New York Times* and *USA Today* bestselling Blueberry Lane Series, which follows the English, Winslow, Rousseau, Story, and Ambler families of Philadelphia; the six-book, bestselling ~a modern fairytale~ series; and several other stand-alone novels and novellas, including the critically acclaimed, 2018 RITA© nominated, *USA Today* bestselling contemporary romance *Unloved, a love story*.

Katy's first modern fairytale romance, *The Vixen and the Vet*, was nominated for a RITA® in 2015 and won the 2015 Kindle Book Award for romance. Katy's *The English Brothers Boxed Set*, Books #1–4, hit the *USA Today* bestseller list in 2015, and her Christmas story, *Marrying Mr. English*, appeared on the list a week later. In May 2016, Katy's Blueberry Lane collection, *The Winslow Brothers Boxed Set*, Books #1–4, became a *New York Times* e-book bestseller.

Katy's books are available in English, French, Italian, Polish, Portuguese, and Turkish. Her books soon will be available in German and Hebrew.

Katy lives in the relative wilds of northern Fairfield County, Connecticut, where her writing room looks out at the woods, and her husband, two children, two dogs, and one Blue Tonkinese cat create just enough cheerful chaos to remind her that the very best love stories begin at home.

Sign up for Katy's newsletter today.

Connect with Katy

Katy LOVES connecting with her readers and answers every e-mail, message, tweet, and post personally! Connect with Katy!